P9-CMX-466

"Marry me."

Reagan blinked. Blinked again. Surely, he... No, he couldn't have possibly...

"E-excuse me?"

"Marry me," he repeated, his jade gaze steady, his expression solemn. Determined.

Oh God. He'd finally cracked under the pressure from the trouble at Wingate. What other explanation could there be?

"Ezekiel..."

"Hear me out. Please."

He sounded sane. Calm, even. The man had just proposed to her—if she could actually call his demand a proposal. She'd suddenly plummeted into an alternate universe where Ezekiel-damn-Wingate had ordered her to become his wife.

All manners flew out the window in extreme circumstances like this.

And she was really considering this...proposition.

* * *

Trust Fund Fiancé by Naima Simone is part of the Texas Cattleman's Club: Rags to Riches series.

Dear Reader,

The Texas Cattleman's Club. Can I just lose the professional author demeanor for a second and go all fangirl? OMG! *Whew*. Okay, thank you. I'm back. I've been a fan of this long-running series for years, and to now have the chance to write for it? Prepare yourself. Another fangirl scream ahead...

One of my favorite tropes is marriage of convenience. And in *Trust Fund Fiancé*, TCC member and marketing VP Ezekiel "Zeke" Holloway and Royal socialite Reagan Sinclair agree to a union that benefits them both. Reagan wants to access her trust fund, while Zeke finds he can help a friend when he feels completely helpless to aid his family's steady and public decline into ruin. Besides, a whirlwind fairy-tale love story will only grant the Wingates some much-needed positive press. But what neither Zeke nor Reagan count on is their marriage of convenience becoming *very* inconvenient because of that pesky lust and feelings. Oh, aaaall the feelings. But I can honestly say what I loved most about writing this book was writing the journey of two hurt, less-than-perfect people as they find healing and love.

I hope you enjoy my first ever Texas Cattleman's Club book! Even more, I hope you fall in love with Zeke and Reagan just as I did.

Happy reading!

Naima

NAIMA SIMONE

TRUST FUND FIANCÉ

If you purchased this book without a cover you should be aware
that this book is stolen property. It was reported as "unsold and
destroyed" to the publisher, and neither the author nor the
publisher has received any payment for this "stripped book."

Special thanks and acknowledgment are
given to Naima Simone for her contribution to
the Texas Cattleman's Club: Rags to Riches
miniseries.

DESIRE™

Recycling programs
for this product may
not exist in your area.

ISBN-13: 978-1-335-20931-3

Trust Fund Fiancé

Copyright © 2020 by Harlequin Books S.A.

All rights reserved. No part of this book may be used or reproduced in any
manner whatsoever without written permission except in the case of brief
quotations embodied in critical articles and reviews.

This is a work of fiction. Names, characters, places and incidents
are either the product of the author's imagination or are used fictitiously.
Any resemblance to actual persons, living or dead, businesses,
companies, events or locales is entirely coincidental.

This edition published by arrangement with Harlequin Books S.A.

For questions and comments about the quality of this book,
please contact us at CustomerService@Harlequin.com.

Harlequin Enterprises ULC
22 Adelaide St. West, 40th Floor
Toronto, Ontario M5H 4E3, Canada
www.Harlequin.com

Printed in U.S.A.

USA TODAY bestselling author **Naima Simone**'s love of romance was first stirred by Harlequin books pilfered from her grandmother. Now she spends her days writing sizzling romances with a touch of humor and snark.

She is wife to her own real-life superhero and mother to two awesome kids. They live in perfect domestically challenged bliss in the southern United States.

Books by Naima Simone

Harlequin Desire

Blackout Billionaires

The Billionaire's Bargain
Black Tie Billionaire
Blame It on the Billionaire

Dynasties: Seven Sins

Ruthless Pride

Texas Cattleman's Club: Rags to Riches

Trust Fund Fiancé

Visit her Author Profile page at Harlequin.com, or naimasimone.com, for more titles.

You can also find Naima Simone on Facebook, along with other Harlequin Desire authors, at Facebook.com/harlequindesireauthors!

To Gary. 143.

One

A man had a few pleasures in life.

For Ezekiel "Zeke" Holloway, they included kicking back on the black leather couch in the den of the three-bedroom guesthouse that he and his older brother, Luke, shared on the Wingate family estate. He had an ice-cold beer in one hand, a slice of meat lovers pizza in the other and Pittsburgh playing on the mounted eighty-five-inch flat-screen television. Granted, he might've been born and bred in Texas, but his heart belonged to the Steelers.

And then there was this. He lifted the dark brown cigar with its iconic black-and-red label and studied the smoldering red tip before bringing it to his lips and inhaling. A hint of pepper and chocolate, toasted macadamia nuts and, of course, the dark flavor of cognac. It could be addictive...if he allowed it to be. These cigars cost fifteen thousand dollars a box. Which was why he only permitted himself to enjoy one per month. Not because he couldn't afford to buy more. It was about discipline; he mastered his urges, not vice versa.

And in a world that had suddenly become unfamiliar, cold and uncertain, he needed to believe he could control something in his life. Even if it was when he smoked a cigar.

He sighed, bracing a hand on the balcony column and slowly exhaling into the night air. Behind him, the muted hum of chatter filtered through the closed glass doors. Guests gathered in the cavernous parlor behind him. James Harris, current president of the Texas Cattleman's Club—of which Ezekiel was a member—hosted the "small" dinner party. As a highly successful horse breeder in Royal, Texas, and a businessman, James commanded attention without trying. And when he invited a person to his elegant, palatial home, he or she attended.

Even if they would be rubbing elbows with the newly infamous Wingates.

Bringing the cigar to his lips again, Ezekiel stared out into the darkness. Beneath the blanket of the black, star-studded night, he could barely make out the stables, corrals and long stretch of land that made up James's property. He rolled his shoulders, as if the motion could readjust and shift the cumbersome burden of worry, anger and, yes, fear that seemed to hang around his neck like an albatross. It was ludicrous, but he could practically feel the hushed murmurs crawl over his skin through his black dinner jacket and white shirt like the many legs of a centipede. He could massage his chest and still nothing would alleviate the weight of the censure—the press of the guilty verdicts already cast his and his family's way.

Not even the influence and support of James Harris could lessen that.

Lucky for Ezekiel and his family that the denizens of Royal high society hungered for a party invitation from James more than they wanted to outright ostracize the Wingates.

Ezekiel snorted, his lips twisting around the cigar. Thank God for small favors.

"And here I thought I'd found the perfect escape hatch."

Ezekiel jerked his head to the side at the husky, yet very feminine drawl. His mouth curved into a smile. And not the polite, charming and utterly fake one he'd worn all evening. Instead, true affection wound through him like a slowly unfurling ribbon.

Reagan Sinclair glided forward out of the shadows and into the dim glow radiating from the beveled glass balcony doors. It was enough to glimpse her slender but curvaceous body. The high thrust of her small but firm breasts. The fingertip-itching dip of her waist and intriguing swell of her hips. As she drew nearer to him and a scent that reminded him of honeysuckle and cream teased his nostrils, he castigated himself.

At twenty-six, Reagan was only four years his junior, but she was good friends with his cousin Harley, and he'd known her most of her life. She was as "good girl" as they came, with her flawless pedigree and traditional upbringing. Which meant she had no business being out here with him in his current frame of mind.

Not when the dark, hungry beast he usually hid behind carefree, wide grins and wry jokes clawed closer to the surface.

Not when the only thing that usually satisfied that animal was a willing woman and hot, dirty sex. No... *fucking*.

Ezekiel blew out a frustrated breath. Yes, he'd had sex, but made love to a woman? No, he hadn't done that in eight long years.

If he had any sense or the morals that most believed he didn't possess, he would put out his cigar, gently grasp her by the elbow and escort her back to her parents. Away from him. He should—

Reagan touched him.

Just the feel of her slim, delicate hand on his biceps was like a cooling, healing balm. It calmed the anger, the fear. Leashed the hunger. At least so he could meet her thickly lashed, entirely too-innocent eyes and not imagine seeing them darken with a greedy lust that he placed there.

"I know why I'm hiding," he drawled, injecting a playfulness he was far from feeling into his voice. "What's your excuse?"

Those eyes, the color of the delicious chicory coffee his mother used to have shipped from New Orleans, softened, understanding somehow making them more beautiful. And horrible.

He glanced away.

On the pretense of finishing his smoke, he shifted to the side, inserting space between them. Not that he could escape that damn scent that seemed even headier with her so close. Or the sharp-as-a-razor's-edge cheekbones. Or the lush, downright impropriety of her mouth. The smooth bronze of her skin that damn near gleamed…

You've known her since she was a girl. You have no business thinking of her naked, sweating and straining beneath you.

Dammit. He narrowed his gaze on the moon-bleached vista of James's ranch. His dick wasn't having any of that reasoning though. Too bad. He had enough of a shit storm brewing in his life, in his family, in Wingate Enterprises. He refused to add screwing Reagan Sinclair to it.

In a life full of selfish decisions, that might be the cherry on top of his asshole sundae.

And regardless of what some people might think, he possessed lines he didn't cross. A sense of honor that had been drilled into him by his family before he'd even been old enough to understand what the word meant. And as a little dented and battered as the Wingate name might be right now, they were still Wingates.

That meant something here in Royal.

It meant something to him.

"Let's see." She pursed her lips and tapped a fingernail against the full bottom curve. "Should I start alphabetically? A, avoiding my parents introducing me to every single man here between the ages of twenty-two and eighty-two. B, boring small talk about the unseasonably hot summer—it's Texas, mind you—gel versus acrylic nails and, my personal favorite, whether MTV really did need a reboot of *The Hills*. Which, the only answer to that is no. And C, karma—I avoided every one of Tracy Drake's calls last week because the woman is a terrible gossip. And now I find out that I'm seated next to her at dinner."

He snorted. "I'm pretty sure karma starts with a *K*," he said, arching an eyebrow.

"I know." She shrugged a slim shoulder, a smile riding one corner of her mouth. "I couldn't think of anything for *C*."

Their soft laughter rippled on the night air, and for the first time since arriving this evening, the barbed tension inside him loosened.

"And I just needed air that didn't contain politics, innuendo or cigar smoke," she continued. The velvet tone called to mind tangled, sweaty sheets at odds with her perfectly styled hair and immaculately tailored, strapless cocktail dress that spoke of unruffled poise. Even as Ezekiel's rebellious brain conjured up images of just how much he *could* ruffle her poise, she slid him a sidelong glance. "One out of three isn't bad."

Again, the miraculous happened, and he chuckled. *Enjoying* her. "I know it would be the gentlemanly thing to put this out..." he lifted the offending item between them "...but it's one of my few vices—"

"Just a few?" she interrupted, a dimple denting one of her cheeks.

"And I'm going to savor it," he finished, shooting her a mock frown for her cheekiness. Cute cheekiness. "Besides, no one in there would accuse me of being a gentleman."

Dammit. He hadn't meant to let that slip. Not the words and definitely not the bitterness. He was the carefree jokester of the Holloway brothers. He laughed and teased; he *didn't* brood. But these last few months had affected them all. Turned them into people they sometimes didn't recognize.

Talk and accusations of corruption and fraud did that to a person.

So did a headlong tumble from a pedestal, only to discover those you'd known for years were only wearing the masks of friends, hiding their true faces underneath. Vultures. Sharks.

Predators.

He forced a smile, and from the flash of sadness that flickered across her lovely features, the twist of his lips must've appeared as fake as it felt. For a moment, anger that wasn't directed at himself for fucking caring about the opinions of others blazed within him. Now it was presently aimed at her. At her pity that he hated. That he probably deserved.

And he resented that more.

"Gentlemen are highly overrated," she murmured, before he could open his mouth and let something mean and regrettable pour out. Her quiet humor snuffed out the flame of his fury. Once more the utter *calm* of her presence washed over him, and part of him wanted to soak in it until the grime of the past few months disappeared from his skin, his mind, his heart. "Besides, I want to hear more about some of these vices."

"No, you don't," he contradicted.

Unable to resist, he snagged a long, loose wave resting on her shoulder. He pinched it, testing the thickness, the silkiness of it between his thumb and forefinger. It didn't require much imagination to guess how it would feel whispering across his bare chest, his abdomen. His thighs. Soft. Ticklish. And so damn erotic, his cock already hardened in anticipation. As if scalded by both the sensation and the too-hot mental image, he released his grip, tucking the rebellious hand in his pants pocket.

Giving himself time to banish his impure thoughts toward his cousin's friend, he brought the cigar to his mouth. Savoring the flavor of chocolate and cognac. Letting it obscure the illusory taste of honeysuckle, vanilla and female flesh.

"You're too young for that discussion," he added, silently cursing the roughness of his tone.

"Oh really?" She tilted her head to the side. "You do know I'm only four years younger than you, right? Or are you having trouble with remembering things at your advanced old age of thirty?"

He narrowed his eyes on her. "Brat," he rumbled.

"Not the first time I've heard that," she said, something murkier than the shadows they stood in shifting in her eyes. But then she smiled, and the warmth of it almost convinced him that the emotion had been a trick of the dark. "So don't hold back. And start with the good stuff. And by good, I mean very, very bad."

He exhaled, studying her through the plume of fragrant smoke he blew through slightly parted lips. "You think you can handle my bad, Ray?" he taunted, deliberately using the masculine nickname that used to make her roll her eyes in annoyance.

Anything to remind him that he'd once caught her and Harley practicing kissing on his cousin's pillows. That she used to crush on boy bands with more synthesizers than talent. That he'd wiped her tears and offered to pound on the little shit that had bullied her on the playground over something she couldn't change— her skin color.

Anything to reinforce that she wasn't one of the women whose front doors would witness his walks of shame.

With an arch of a brow, she leaned forward so she couldn't help but inhale the evaporating puff. "Try me," she whispered.

A low, insistent throb pulsed low in his gut, and his abs clenched, as if grasping for that familiar but somehow different grip of desire.

Desire. For Reagan? Wrong. So damn wrong.

Coward, a sibilant voice hissed at him. And he mentally flipped it off, shifting backward and leaning a shoulder against a stone column.

"Let's see," he said, valiantly injecting a lazy note of humor into his voice. "I can put away an entire meat lovers pizza by myself *and* not use a coaster for my beer. I'm unreasonably grouchy if I'm awake before the god-awful hour of seven o'clock. Especially if there's no coffee to chase away my pain. And—this one I'm kind of embarrassed to admit—I buy at least five pairs of socks every month. Apparently, my dryer is a portal to a world where mismatched socks are some kind of special currency. And since I can't abide not matching, I'm constantly a spendthrift on new pairs. There. You now know all of my immoralities."

A beat of silence, and then, "Really?"

He smirked. "Really," he replied, then jerked his chin up. "Your turn. Regale me with all of your sins, little Ray."

As he'd expected, irritation glinted in her chocolate eyes. "I have no idea how I can follow that, but here goes." He huffed out a low chuckle at the thick sarcasm coating her words. "Every night, I slip downstairs after everyone has gone to bed and have a scotch by myself. No one to judge me, you see? Since my nightly ritual could be early signs of me becoming an alcoholic like my uncle James. What else?"

She hummed, trailing her fingertips over her collarbone, her lashes lowering in a pretense of deep thought. But Ezekiel knew better. She'd already given this a lot of consideration. Had already catalogued her perceived faults long before this conversation.

Acid swirled in his stomach, creeping a path up his chest. He straightened from his lounge against the pillar, prepared to nip this in the bud, but she forestalled him by speaking again. And though a part of him yearned to tell her to stop, to warn her not to say another word, the other part... Yeah, that section wanted to hear how imperfect she was. Craved it. Because it made him feel less alone.

More human.

God, he was such a selfish prick.

And yet, he listened.

"I hate roses. I mean, *loathe* them. Which is important because my mother loves them. And every morning there are fresh bouquets of them delivered to the house for every room, including the kitchen. And every day I fight the urge to knock one down just to watch them scatter across the floor in a mess of water, petals and thorns. Because I'm petty like that. And finally..."

She inhaled, turning to look at him, those eyes, stark and utterly beautiful in their intensity, pinning him to his spot against the railing. "Once a month, I drive over to Joplin and visit the bars and restaurants to find a man to take to a hotel for a night. We have hot, filthy sex and then I leave and return home to be Royal socialite darling Reagan Sinclair again."

Heat—blistering hot and scalding—blasted through

him, punching him in the chest and searing him to the bone. Jesus, did she just…? *Holy fuck.* Lust ate at him. Lust…and horror. Not because she took charge of her own sexuality. It was a twisted and unfair double standard, how men like him could escort woman after woman on his arm, and screw many more, with only an elbow nudge or knowing wink from society. But a woman doing the same thing? Especially one of Reagan's status? Hell no. So for her to take her pleasure into her own hands? He didn't fault her for it.

But the thought of her trolling those establishments filled with drunk men? Some man who wouldn't have an issue with not taking the utmost care with her? Of potentially hurting her? That sent fear spiking through him, slaying him.

And then underneath the horror swirled something else. Something murkier. Edgier. And better off not being unearthed or examined too closely.

"Reagan…" he whispered.

"Relax," she scoffed, flicking a hand toward his face. "I made the last one up. But turnabout is fair play since I'm almost eighty-two percent sure you were lying to me about at least one of yours. Maybe two."

He froze. Stared at her. Stunned…and speechless. Mirror emotions—hilarity and anger—battled it out within him. He didn't know whether to strangle her for taking twenty years off his life… Or double over with laughter loud enough to bring people rushing through those balcony doors.

"That wasn't very nice," he finally muttered, his fingers in danger of snapping his prized cigar in half. "And payback is not only a bitch but a vengeful one."

"I'm shaking in my Jimmy Choos," she purred.

And this time, he couldn't hold back the bark of laughter. Or the *goodness* of it. Surrendering to the need to touch her, even if in a platonic manner, he moved forward and slipped an arm around her shoulders, hugging Reagan into his side like he used to do when she'd worn braces and friendship bracelets.

There was nothing girlish about the body that aligned with his. Nothing pure about the stirrings in his chest and gut…then *lower*. A new strain took up residence in his body. One that had nothing to do with the whispers and gossiping awaiting him inside. This tension had everything to do with her light, teasing scent, the slender hand branding his chest, the firm, beautiful breasts that pressed against him.

Still, he squeezed her close before releasing her.

"Thank you, Reagan," he murmured.

She studied him, nothing coy in that straightforward gaze. "You're welcome," she said, not pretending to misunderstand him. Another thing he'd always liked about her. Reagan Sinclair didn't play games. At least not with him. "That's what friends are for. And regardless how it appears right now, you have friends, Zeke," she said softly, using his nickname.

He stared down at her. At the kindness radiating from her eyes. An admonishment to hide that gentle heart of hers from people—from *him*—hovered on his tongue. The need to contradict her skulked right behind it.

Instead, he set his cigar down on an ashtray some enterprising soul had left outside on a wrought iron table. He wasn't an animal, so he didn't stub it out like a cigarette, but left it there to burn out on its own. In a while, he'd come back to dispose of it.

Turning to Reagan, he crooked his arm and waited. Without hesitation, she slid hers through his, but as they turned, the balcony door swung open and Douglas Sinclair stepped out.

Ezekiel knew the older man, as he was a member of the TCC. Tall, lanky and usually wearing his signature giant Stetson, he could've been an African-American version of the Marlboro Man. He shared the same brown eyes as his daughter, and right now those eyes were trained on them—or rather on Reagan's arm tucked into his.

A moment later, Douglas lifted his gaze and met Ezekiel's. Her father didn't voice his displeasure, but Ezekiel didn't miss the slight narrowing of his eyes or the barely-there flattening of his mouth. No, Douglas Sinclair was too polite to tell Ezekiel to get his hands off his daughter. But he stated it loud and clear just the same. Ezekiel might be a TCC member as well, but that didn't mean the traditional, reserved gentleman would want his precious daughter anywhere near him.

Not when Ezekiel's family had been accused of falsifying inspections on the jets that WinJet, a subsidiary of Wingate Enterprises, manufactured. Not when three of their workers had been injured on the job because of a fire in one of the manufacturing plants due to a faulty sprinkler system. Not when they'd been sued for those injuries because those inspections hadn't been up-to-date as the reports had stated.

Even as VP of marketing for Wingate Enterprises, Ezekiel had found it damn near impossible to spin this smear on their name. No one wanted to do business with a company so corrupt it would place profit above their employees' welfare. Not that his family was guilty of this sin. But public perception was *everything*.

And while most of the club members had stood behind the Wingates, Douglas hadn't been vocal in his belief in their innocence.

So it was no wonder the man didn't look pleased to find his daughter hiding in the dark with Ezekiel.

Not that Ezekiel could blame him. Reagan shouldn't be out here with him. But not for the reasons her father harbored.

"Reagan," Douglas said, one hand remaining on the door and holding it open. "Your mother has been looking for you. It's almost time for dinner, and Devon Granger is eager to escort you into the dining room since you'll be sitting next to him."

Ezekiel caught the soft sigh that escaped her, and felt the tension invade her slender frame. But when she spoke, her tone remained as soft and respectful as any dutiful daughter to a father she loved and revered.

"Thanks, Dad. I'll be there in a moment," she murmured.

"I'll wait for you," came his implacable reply.

If possible, she stiffened even more, but her lovely features didn't reflect her irritation. Still, anger for the other man's high-handedness kindled in Ezekiel's chest. She was a grown woman, for God's sake, not a wayward toddler. His arm tautened, trapping hers in the crook of his elbow. Next to him, Reagan tipped her head up, glancing at him.

What the hell are you doing?

Deliberately, he relaxed his body, releasing her and stepping to the side.

"It was nice seeing you again, Reagan," Ezekiel said.

Switching his attention to Douglas, he gave the man an abrupt nod. "You, too, Douglas."

"Ezekiel." Then, extending his hand to his daughter, he added, "Reagan."

She glided forward, sliding her hand into her father's. She didn't shoot one last look over her shoulder at him. Didn't toss him another of her gentle, teasing smiles or a final farewell. Instead, she disappeared through the door, leaving him in darkness once more.

And yeah, it was for the best.

No matter her father's reasons for not wanting to leave her alone with Ezekiel, his concerns were valid. If anyone else had noticed that she stood alone with him in the shadows, the rumors would've burned like a brushfire.

And the longer they remained enclosed in the dark, the harder it would've become for him to remember that she was off-limits to him. Because of their history. Because she was too good for him. Because her parents were seeking out a suitable man for her.

And Ezekiel—a man with a slowly crumbling business empire and more emotional baggage than the airplanes WinJet manufactured—wasn't a good bet.

Not a good bet at all.

Two

Reagan jogged up the four shallow stone steps to her family's Pine Valley mansion. Once she reached the portico that stretched from one end of the front of the house to the other, she stopped, her chest rising and falling on deep, heavy breaths. Turning, she flattened a palm against one of the columns and, reaching for her foot, pulled it toward her butt in a stretch.

God, she detested running. Not even the beautiful scenery of the well-manicured streets and gorgeous multimillion-dollar homes of their upscale, gated community could distract her from the burn in her thighs, the hitch in her chest or the numbing boredom of it. But regardless, she exited her house every morning at 7:00 a.m. to jog past the mansions where Royal high society slept, the clubhouse larger than most people's homes, the Olympic-size pool that called her to take a refreshing dip, and the eighteen-hole golf course. The chore wasn't about pleasure or even staying healthy or retaining a particular dress size.

It was about discipline.

Everyone in this world had to do things they disliked. But likes and dislikes didn't compare to loyalty, sacrifice, love... And though whether or not she jogged every morning had nothing to do with those ideals, the exercise served as a reminder of what happened when a person lost control. When they allowed their selfish wants to supersede everything else that mattered.

Her reminder.

Her *penance*.

Didn't matter. She would continue to do it. Even if running never became easier. Never ceased to make her feel like she wanted to collapse and call on the Lord to end her suffering.

Moments later, as she finished her stretching, the door behind her opened. Her father stepped out, and once again that familiar and so complicated flood of emotion poured through her as it did whenever she was in Douglas Sinclair's presence.

Awe. Reverence. Guilt. Shame. Anger. Resentment. *Love.*

She was a murky, tangled hodgepodge of feelings when it came to her father.

"Good morning, Dad," she greeted, straightening from a deep lunge.

"Reagan." He peered down at her, his customary Stetson not hiding the frown wrinkling his brow. "Out running again, I see." He tsked, shaking his head. "We have a perfectly good gym downstairs with top-of-the-line equipment, and yet you insist on gallivanting around the neighborhood."

Gallivanting. If his obvious disapproval didn't grate on her nerves like a cheese grinder, she would've snorted at the old-fashioned word. But that was her father. Old-fashioned. Traditional. Conservative. All nice words to say he liked things done a certain way. Including not having his daughter jog around their posh neighborhood in athletic leggings and a sports tank top. Modest women didn't show their bodies in that fashion.

Unfortunately for him, she couldn't run in a high-waisted gown with a starched collar.

Forcing a smile to her lips, she said, "I'm hardly parading around, Dad. I'm exercising." Before he could respond to that, she pressed on. "Headed into the office?" she asked, already knowing the answer.

She could set her watch by him. Breakfast at 7:00 a.m. Leave for the law office at 7:45. To Douglas Sinclair, integrity was a religion. And that included being accountable to his time and his clients.

"Yes." He glanced down at his watch. "I left a message with your mother, but now that I'm seeing you, please don't forget that we have dinner plans tonight. The Grangers are coming over, and you need to be here. On time," he emphasized. More like commanded. "I understand your committee work is important, but not more so than honoring your commitments. I expect you to be here and dressed at six sharp."

He doesn't mean to be condescending. Or controlling. Or patronizing. He loves you.

Silently, she ran the refrain through her head. Over and over until the words melded together. He didn't know about her work at the girls' home in Colonial

County. It wasn't his fault he saw her through the lens of another era—outdated traditions, unobtainable expectations…

A disappointed father.

"Devon is attending with his parents. So you need to be at your best tonight," he continued. "You seemed to show interest in him at James Harris's get-together last week. You two talked quite a bit at dinner. With his family, his position in his father's real estate development company and business connections, he would make an ideal husband."

Jesus. This again. Reagan just managed not to pinch the bridge of her nose and utter profanity that would have her father gasping.

He just didn't stop. Didn't give her a chance to breathe. To make a single decision for herself.

Since she'd turned twenty-six five months ago, he'd been on this relentless campaign to see her married. Just as her brother had. As her sister had only a year ago.

It was all so ridiculous. So damn antiquated. And stifling. She could find her own goddamn husband, *if* she wanted one.

Which she didn't.

She loved her parents; they'd always provided a more-than-comfortable home, the best schools, a good, solid family life. But her father was definitely the head of the household, and Henrietta Sinclair, though the mediator and often the voice of reason, very rarely went against him. While the relationship might work well for them, Reagan couldn't imagine allowing a man to have that much control over her.

Besides, she'd done that once. Let a man consume

her world—*be* her world. And that had ended in a spectacularly disastrous display.

No, she didn't want a husband who'd give her a home and his shadow to live in.

"Dad, I appreciate your concern, but I wish you and Mom would stop…with the matchmaking attempts. I've told both of you that marriage isn't a priority for me right now." If ever. "I'll show up for dinner tonight, but don't expect a love match. While Devon Granger may be nice and husband material, he's not *my* husband material."

Poor Devon. His most interesting quality had been providing a distraction from Tracy Drake, seated on her other side. And since the notorious gossip had spotted Ezekiel Holloway following Reagan and her father back into the house within moments, she'd been chock-full of questions and assumptions. The woman had missed her calling as a CIA agent.

Her father scoffed. "A love match." He shook his head, exasperation clearly etched into his expression. "Don't be ridiculous. I'm not anticipating a proposal at the end of the evening. I just want you to at least give him a chance." He glanced at his watch again, impatience vibrating off him. "As your father, I want to see you happy, settled. With a husband who can provide for you." He flicked the hand not holding his briefcase. "Don't be naive, Reagan. Do you think people aren't talking about the fact that your sister, who is three years younger than you, is already married? That maybe there's something—"

"I'm not Christina," she interrupted him, voice quiet and steady in spite of how *hurt* trembled through her like a wind-battered leaf. She knew what lay on the other side of that *something*. And she didn't need to hear him state how their friends and associates whispered if she was faulty in some way. Or to hear the unspoken concern in her father's voice that he wondered the same thing. Except swap out *faulty* for *broken*.

"I'm not Doug either," she added, mentioning her older brother. "I have my own aspirations, and marriage isn't even at the top of that list."

"God, not that again—"

"And if you would just release the money Gran left me, I could further those goals. And a life of my choosing. Filled with *my* decisions," she finished, tracing the faint childhood scar on her collarbone. Trying—and failing—not to let his annoyed dismissal of her wants puncture her pride and self-esteem. By now, both resembled a barroom corkboard, riddled with holes from so many well-meaning but painful darts.

"We've been over this, and the answer is still no," he ground out. "Your grandmother loved you so much she left that inheritance to you, but she also added the stipulation for a reason. And we both know why, Reagan."

We both know why... We both know why...

The words rang between them in the already warm morning air.

A warning.

An indictment.

Oh yes, how could she forget why her beloved grandmother, who had left her enough money to make her an instant millionaire, had added one provision in her will? Reagan couldn't access the inheritance until she either married a suitable man or turned thirty years old.

In order to be fully independent, to manage her own life, she had to chain herself to a man and hand over that independence or wait four more years before she could...*live*.

It was her punishment, her penance. For rebelling. For not following the Sinclair script. For daring to be less than perfect.

At sixteen, she'd done what most teenage girls did— she'd fallen in love. But she'd fallen hard. Had been consumed by the blaze of first love with this nineteen-year-old boy that her parents hadn't approved of. So when they'd forbidden her to see him, she'd sneaked around behind their backs. She'd offered everything to him—her loyalty, her heart, her virginity.

And had ended up pregnant.

Understandably, her parents had been horrified and disappointed. They'd wanted to send her away, have the baby and give it up for adoption. And Reagan had been determined to keep her unborn daughter or son. But neither of them had their wish. She'd miscarried. And the boy she'd been so certain she'd spend the rest of her life with had disappeared.

The price for her stubborn foolishness had been her utter devastation and her family's trust.

And sometimes...when she couldn't sleep, when her guard was down and she was unable to stop the buffeting of her thoughts and memories, she believed she'd lost some of their love, too.

Over the years, she'd tried to make up for that time by being the obedient, loyal, *perfect* daughter they deserved. It was why she still remained in her childhood home even though, at her age, she should have her own place.

But ten years later, she still caught her mother studying her a little too close when Reagan decided to do something as small as not attend one of her father's events for his law firm. Still glimpsed the concern in Henrietta's eyes when Reagan disagreed with them. At one time Reagan had made her mother physically ill from the worry she'd caused, the pain she'd inflicted with her bad decisions. So to remain under the same roof where Henrietta could keep tabs on her, could assure herself that her daughter wasn't once again self-destructing... It was a small cost. She owed her parents that much.

Because in her family's eyes, she would never be more than that misguided, impetuous teen. She was her family's well-kept, dirty little secret, a cautionary tale for her sister.

The weight of the knowledge bore down on her so hard, her shoulders momentarily bowed. But she'd become the poster child for *fake it until you make it*. Sucking in an inaudible deep breath, she tilted her chin up and met her father's dark scrutiny.

"I guess we're at an impasse, then. Again," she tacked on. "Have a great day, Dad."

Turning on her heel, she headed inside the house before he could say something that would unknowingly tear another strip from her heart. She quietly shut the door behind her, leaning against it. Taking a moment to recover from another verbal and emotional battle with her father.

Sighing, she straightened and strode toward the rear of the house and the kitchen for a cold bottle of water. The thickly sweet scent of flowers hit her seconds before she spied the vase of lush flowers with their dark red petals.

I hate roses. I mean, loathe them... Every morn-

ing there are fresh bouquets of them delivered to the house... And every day I fight the urge to knock one down just to watch them scatter across the floor in a mess of water, petals and thorns. Because I'm petty like that.

The murmured admission whispered through her mind, dragging her from the here-and-now back to that shadowed balcony a little over a week ago.

Back to Ezekiel Holloway.

She drew to a halt in the middle of the hallway, her eyes drifting shut. The memories slammed into her. Not that they had a great distance to travel. He and their interlude hadn't been far from her mind since that night.

Zeke.

She'd once called him that before she'd fallen in love, then fallen out of favor with her family. Before her childhood had ended in a crash-and-burn that she still bore the scars from.

Before she'd erected this imaginary wall of plexiglass between her and people that protected her. But she'd slipped up at the dinner party. The pseudo-intimacy of the dark coaxing her into falling into old, familiar patterns.

An image of Zeke wavered, then solidified on the black screen of her eyelids.

Lovely.

Such an odd word to describe a man. Especially one who stood nearly a foot taller than her and possessed a lean but powerful, wide-shouldered body that stirred both desire and envy. Regardless, her description was still accurate. He'd been beautiful as a teen, but the years had honed that masculine beauty, experience had added an edge to it. The dark hair cut close to his head only emphasized the stunning bone structure that reminded her of cliffs sculpted to razor sharpness by wind and rain. A formidable face prettied by a firm mouth almost indecent in its fullness and a silken, neatly cropped beard framing his sinful lips.

Then there were those eyes.

The color of new spring grass warmed by the sun. Light green and striking against skin the color of brown sugar.

Yes, he was a lovely man. An intimidating man. A powerful, *desirable* man.

Zeke was a temptation that lured her to step closer. To stroke her fingers over that dark facial hair that would abrade her skin like rug burn. To pet him like the sleek but lethal panther he reminded her of. To taste that brown sugar skin and see if it was as sweet as it looked.

But he was also a warning sign that blinked *Danger!* in neon red. Not since Gavin, her teenage love who'd abandoned her and broken her young heart, had she been the least bit tempted to lose control again. None had poked that curious shifting inside her, stirred the dormant need to be...wild. To act without thought of consequence. To throw herself into an ocean of feeling and willingly go under.

Ten minutes with Ezekiel and that tingle deep inside her crackled, already singeing the tight ropes tying down that part of her. The last time she'd loosened those bindings, she'd hurt her family terribly.

No, she couldn't allow that to happen again.

So, though part of her had railed at her father's autocratic behavior that night, the other half had been relieved as she'd walked back into the house and away from him. Okay, maybe Zeke had infiltrated her dreams since then. And in those dreams, she'd remained on the shadowed balcony. He also hadn't stopped with touching her hair. And maybe when she woke, her body trembled from unfulfilled pleasure. A pleasure that left her empty and aching.

It was okay. Because they were only dreams relegated to the darkest part of night where secret desires resided.

Didn't matter. Not when her mind and heart agreed on one indelible truth.

Ezekiel Holloway spelled trouble with a capital *T*.

Best she remembered that.

And the possible consequences if she dared to forget.

Three

Ezekiel hunkered down on the still green grass, balancing on the balls of his feet. The late-afternoon sun didn't penetrate this corner of the cemetery where the Southern live oak's branches spread wide and reached toward the clear, blue sky. The tree provided shade over the marble headstone. And as he traced the etched lettering that hadn't yet faded after eight years, the stone was cool to the touch. If he closed his eyes and lost himself like he did in those nebulous, gray moments just before fully wakening, he could imagine another name inscribed on the marker.

Not Melissa Evangeline Drake.

Heaving a sigh that sounded weary to his own ears, he rose, shoving his hands into his pants pockets, never tearing his gaze from the monument that failed to encapsulate the woman who had once held his heart in her petite hands.

A name. Dates of her birth and way-too-soon death. Daughter, sister, friend.

Not *fiancée*. Not *the other half of Ezekiel Holloway's soul*.

And he didn't blame them. After all, he'd only had her in his life four short years, while they'd had twenty-two. She belonged to them more than she ever did to him. But for a while, she'd been solely his. His joy. His life. His *everything*. And she'd been snatched away by a man who'd decided getting behind a wheel while drunk off his ass had been a good idea.

One moment, they'd been happy, planning their future together. The next, he'd received a devastating phone call from her father that she was gone. The only merciful blessing had been that she'd died on impact when the drunk had plowed into the driver's side of her car.

And a part of him had died with her that night. The part that had belonged to her and only her.

"I can't believe it's been eight years to the day since I lost you," he said to the tombstone, pausing as if it could answer.

Most days, he struggled to remember what her voice sounded like. Time might not heal all wounds, but it damn sure dimmed the details he tried to clutch close and hoard like a miser hiding his precious gold.

"I have to tell you this is not the anniversary I imagined we'd have." He huffed out a humorless chuckle. "I tried to call your parents yesterday and this morning, but they didn't answer. I understand," he quickly added, careful not to malign the parents they'd both adored.

"Losing you devastated them. And I'm a reminder of that pain. Still…" He paused, his jaw locking, trying to trap in the words he could only admit here, to his dead fiancée. "I miss them. I had Aunt Ava and Uncle Trent after Mom and Dad died, but your folks… They were good to me. And I hated losing them so soon after you. But yeah, I don't blame them."

They all had to do what they needed to move on, to return to the world of the living.

He'd thrown himself into work and any kind of activity that had taunted fate to come for him again—skydiving, rock climbing, rappelling.

And the women. The daredevil adventures might burn off the restlessness, but they couldn't touch the loneliness. The emptiness. Only sex did that. Even if it was only for those few blessed hours when he was inside a woman and pleasure provided that sweet oblivion. Adrenaline and sex. They were his sometime drugs of choice. Temporary highs.

When those were his ways of coping with the past, the loss, how could he hold it against the Drakes that they'd chosen to cauterize him from their lives?

"I know it's been several months since I've visited, and so damn much has happened since then—"

"Zeke?"

He jerked his head up and, spying the woman standing on the other side of the grave, blinked. Surely his brain had conjured the image to taunt him. How else could he explain Reagan Sinclair here in this cemetery?

Unbidden and against his will, his gaze traveled down her slender frame clothed in a pale-yellow dress that bared her shoulders and arms and crisscrossed over her breasts. For a second, he lingered over the V that offered him a hint of smooth, rounded flesh before continuing his perusal over the long, flowing skirt that brushed the tips of her toes and the grass. She resembled a goddess, golden, lustrous brown skin and long hair twisted into a braid that rested over one shoulder. And when he lifted his scrutiny to her face, he couldn't help but skim the vulnerable, sensual curves of her mouth, the almost haughty tilt of her cheekbones and the coffee-brown eyes.

Silently, he swore, yanking his regard back to the headstone. And hating himself for detecting details about this woman he had no business, no *right* to notice. Especially standing over the grave of the woman he'd loved.

"Hey," she softly greeted him, blissfully unaware of the equal parts resentment and need that clawed at him.

"What are you doing here?" he asked, tone harsher than he'd intended. Than she deserved.

But if the question or the delivery offended her, she didn't show it. Instead, she moved closer, and even though he'd thoroughly scrutinized her only moments ago, he just noted the bouquet of vibrant blue-and-white flowers she held. She knelt, her skirt billowing around her, and laid the flowers in front of the gravestone. Straightening, she paused, resting a hand on top of the marble before stepping back. Only then did she meet his gaze.

And in that instant, he was transported back eight years. A lot about the day of Melissa's funeral had been a blur, but how could he have forgotten that it'd been Reagan who'd found him at this very same, freshly covered grave after everyone else had left for the repast at the Drakes'? Reagan who had slipped her hand into his and silently stood next to him, not rushing him to leave, not talking, just…refusing to leave him alone. She might've been his cousin's friend back then, but that day, in those long, dark moments, she'd been his.

He smothered a sigh and dragged a hand down his face, his beard scratching his palm.

"I'm sorry," he murmured. "This day—"

She shook her head, holding up her hand to forestall the rest of his apology. "I understand." She paused. "Does it get any easier?" she asked, voice whisper soft.

Did it? Any other place on any other day, he might've offered his canned and packaged reply of *yes, time is the great healer.* But the words stumbled on his tongue. Then died a defeated death. "Most days, yes. The pain dulls so it doesn't feel as if every breath is like a knife in the chest. But then there are other days when…"

His gaze drifted toward the other side of the cemetery. What his eyes couldn't see, his mind supplied. Two matching headstones, side by side. The people buried there together in death as they'd been determined to be in life.

I feel empty, he silently completed the thought. *Unanchored. Alone. Abandoned.*

He would've denied those words, those feelings if anyone vocalized them to him. Especially his older brother, Luke. But in his head where he couldn't run from his denial?

Well…even if he had the speed of Usain Bolt, he couldn't sprint fast enough to escape himself.

"I forgot your parents were buried here," Reagan said, her voice closer. Her scent nearer, more potent. "I always wondered why they weren't with the rest of the Wingates in their mausoleum."

"Because they weren't Wingates," he replied, still staring off into the distance, squelching the clench of his gut at his explanation. Smothering the unruly and insidious thought that he wasn't one either. That in a family mixed with Wingates and Holloways, he and Luke were still…different.

"My father was a Holloway, Aunt Ava's older brother. He created a bit of a scandal in the family and society when he married my mother, a black woman. But in spite of the derision and ostracization they faced—sometimes within his own family—my parents had a happy marriage. Even if they remained somewhat distant from the rest of the Holloways."

"They were protecting their world," Reagan murmured. "I don't think there's anything wrong with that."

"They were very careful, sheltering. But they still taught us the value of family. When they died in that car crash eleven years ago, Aunt Ava and Uncle Trent took Luke and me in…even though by then, we were both in college and technically adults. They gave us a place to call home when ours had been irrevocably broken."

He turned back to her. "They might have taken us in, and we now work for the family company, but my parents didn't consider themselves Wingates, so Luke and I didn't bury them as ones."

She slowly nodded. Studied him in that calm-as-lake-waters way of hers that still perceived too much. Unlike most people, she didn't seem content with just seeing the charmer, the thrill seeker.

He didn't like it.

But damn if a small part of him didn't hate it either.

"Where will you choose to be buried? The Wingate side or the Holloways?" she mused. But there was nothing casual or easy about the question…or the answer. "God, that's a morbid question. I heard it as soon as I asked it. Still…can't be easy feeling as if you're split in two. Trying to figure out if love or obligation, a debt unpaid, holds you here."

His pulse thudded, echoing in his ears. And inside his chest, the arrow that had struck quivered in agitation.

"What are you doing here?" he asked, abruptly changing the subject away from his family. From his own discomfort and inner demons. "Can't be just to visit Melissa's grave."

That clear inspection didn't waver, but after several seconds, she released him from it, glancing over her shoulder. And he exhaled on a low, deep breath.

"No, my grandmother rests just over there. I come by every other week. It's only been a couple of months since we lost her, so being here…" She shrugged a shoulder. "It brings me more comfort than it does her, I'm sure. But I try to bring enough flowers for her and Melissa."

"Thank you," he said, his palm itching to stroke down the length of her dark brown braid. He slid his hand in his pocket instead. "And I'm sorry about your grandmother." The troubles with WinJet and the fire in the manufacturing plant had consumed him, and he'd been working like a madman since, so he hadn't heard about her death. "I didn't know her, but she must've been very special."

The brief hesitation might not have been caught by most people. But most people weren't paying attention to every breath that passed through Reagan's lips.

"We shared a close bond," she said.

"But?" Ezekiel prodded. "There's definitely a *but* there."

His light teasing didn't produce the effect he'd sought—the lightening of the shadows that had crowded into her gaze.

"But it's difficult to discover the one person you believed loved you unconditionally didn't trust you."

The tone—quiet, almost tranquil—didn't match the words. So one of them was a deception. From personal experience, he'd bet on the tone.

And against his better judgment but to his dick's delight, when he reached out, grasped her chin between his thumb and forefinger and tipped her head back, he had confirmation.

Her eyes. Those magnificent, beautiful eyes couldn't lie. If windows were eyes to the soul, Reagan's were fucking floor-to-ceiling bay windows thrown wide open to the world.

A man could lose himself in them. Step inside and never leave.

With a barely concealed snarl directed at himself, he dropped his arm and just managed not to step back. In retreat. Because that's what it would be. Flight from the need to fall into the pool of those eyes.

He'd had that sensation of drowning before. And he'd willingly dived in. And now the person who was supposed to be there to always keep him afloat lay in the ground at both of their feet.

Fuck it. He took that step back.

"Why do you think she didn't trust you?" he asked, focusing on Reagan and not the fear that scratched at his breastbone.

She released a short, brittle huff. "Think? I know."

Shifting, she gave him her profile, but he caught the slight firming of her lips, the drag of her fingertips across the left side of her collarbone. He narrowed his eyes on the small movement. She'd done that the night of the party. Was it a subconscious tell on her part? He catalogued the detail to take out and analyze later.

"Well, tell me why she didn't trust you, then," he pushed. Gently, but it was still a push. Something inside him—something ephemeral but insatiable—hungered to know more about this woman who had grown up right under his nose but remained this familiar, sexy-as-hell stranger.

"Did you know that I'm a millionaire?" she asked, dodging his question—no, his demand.

Ezekiel nodded. "I'm not surprised. Your father is a very successful—"

"No." She waved a hand, cutting him off. "Not through my father. In my own right, I'm a millionaire. When my grandmother died, she left each of her three grandchildren enough money to never have to worry about being taken care of. But that's the thing. She *did* worry. About me anyway." No breeze kicked up over the quiet cemetery, yet she crossed her arms, clutching her elbows. "She added a stipulation to her will. I can only receive my inheritance when I turn thirty—or marry. And not just any man. A *suitable* man."

Her lips twisted on *suitable*, and he resisted the urge to smooth his thumb over the curve, needing to eradicate the bitterness encapsulated in it. That emotion didn't belong on her—didn't sit right with him.

"The condition doesn't mean she didn't trust you. Maybe she just wanted to make sure you were fully mature before taking on the responsibility and burden that comes with money."

Not that he believed that bullshit. Age didn't matter as much as experience. Hell, there were days he looked in the mirror and expected to glimpse a bent, wizened old man instead of his thirty-year-old self.

"I could accept that if I weren't the only grandchild hit with that proviso. Doug and Christina might both be married, but neither of them had that particular restriction on their inheritance. Just me."

"Why?" he demanded.

Confusion and anger sparked inside him. He was familiar with Reagan's older brother and younger sister, and both were normal, nice people. Maybe a little too nice and, well, boring. But Reagan? She was the perfect image of a Royal socialite—composed, well-mannered and well-spoken, serving on several committees, free of the taint of scandal, reputation beyond reproach. So what the hell?

She didn't immediately reply but stared at him for several long moments. "Most people would've asked what I did to earn that censure."

"I'm not most people, Ray," he growled.

"No, you're not," she murmured, scanning his face, and then, she shook her head. "The why doesn't really matter, does it? What does matter is that at twenty-six, I'm in this holding pattern. Where I can see everyone else enjoying the lives they've carved out for themselves—and I can't move. Either I chain myself to a man I barely know and don't love to access my inheritance. Or I stay here, static for another four years while my own dreams, my own needs and wants wither and die on the vine."

Once more, she'd adopted that placid tone, but this time, Ezekiel caught the bright slashes of hurt, the red tinge of anger underneath it.

"I'm more than just the daughter of Douglas Sinclair. I'm more than just the member of this and that charity committee. Not that I'm denigrating their work. It's just… I want to…be free," she whispered, and he sensed that she hadn't meant for that to slip. For him to hear it.

What did she mean by *free*? Not for the first time, he sensed Reagan's easygoing, friendly mask hid deeper waters. Secrets. He didn't trust secrets. They had a way of turning around and biting a person in the ass. Or knocking a person on it.

"Surely your father can find a way around the will. Especially if it seems to penalize you but not your brother or sister," he argued, his mind already contemplating obtaining a copy of the document and submitting it to Wingate Enterprises's legal department to determine what, if anything, could be done. Some loophole.

"My father doesn't want to find a way around it," she admitted softly, but the confession damn near rocked him back on his heels. "My grandmother did add a codicil. She left it up to my father's discretion to enforce the stipulation. He could release the money to me now or respect her wishes. He's decided he'd rather see me married and settled. *Taken care of*, are his words. As if I'm a child to be passed from one guardian to another like luggage. Or a very fragile package." She chuckled, and the heaviness of it, the *sadness* of it, was a fist pressed against Ezekiel's chest. "That's not far off, actually."

Understanding dawned, and with it came the longing to grab Douglas Sinclair by his throat.

"So that's what the introductions to man after man were about?" he asked.

"The night of James Harris's party?" She nodded. "Yes. And the not-so-subtle invites to our home for dinner. In the last week, there have been three. I feel like a prized car on an auction block. God, it's *humiliating*." For the first time, fire flashed under that calm, and he didn't know whether he wanted to applaud the emotion or draw her into his arms to bank it. He did neither, retaining that careful distance away from her. "I just want to yell *screw it all* and walk away completely. No money, no husband I don't want. But..."

"But family loyalty is a bitch."

A smile ghosted over her lips. "God, yes. And a mean, greedy one to boot."

"Ray." That smile. The awful resignation in it... He couldn't *not* touch her any longer. Crossing the small distance he'd placed between them, he cupped the back of her neck, drawing her close. Placing a kiss to the side of her head, he murmured, "I'm sorry, sweetheart. Family can be our biggest blessing and our heaviest burden."

Brushing his lips over her hair one last time, he dropped his arm and shifted backward again. Ignoring how soft her hair had been against his mouth. Or how his palm itched with the need to reshape itself around her nape again. How he resisted the urge to rub his hand against his leg to somehow erase the feel of her against his skin. "Whatever you decide, make sure it's the best decision for you. This life is entirely too short to deal with regrets."

Her lashes lowered, but not before he caught a glint of emotion in her eyes.

Oh yes. Secrets definitely dwelled there.

"Regrets," she repeated in her low, husky tone. "Yes. Wouldn't want those." Shaking her head, she smiled, but it didn't reach the gaze he stared down into. "I need to go. A meeting. Take care of yourself, Zeke," she said.

With a small wave, she turned and strode down the cemented path, her hips a gentle sway beneath the flowing material of her dress. Tearing his regard from her slender, curvaceous form, he returned it to the grave in front of him. But his mind remained with the woman who'd just walked away from him and not the one lying in the ground at his feet.

I chain myself to a man I barely know and don't love to access my inheritance.

I stay here, static for another four years while my own dreams, my own needs and wants wither and die on the vine.

Her words whirled in his head like a raging storm, its winds refusing to die down. And in the midst of it was his own advice.

This life is entirely too short to deal with regrets.

He should know; he had so many of them. Not calling his parents and telling them he loved them more often. Not being more insistent that Melissa spend the night at his house instead of driving home that night. Not letting his uncle Trent know how much he appreciated all that he'd done for Luke and Ezekiel before he died.

Not being able to turn this WinJet disaster around for the company.

Yeah, he had many regrets.

But… The thoughts in his head spun harder, faster.

Reagan didn't want to shackle herself to a man she barely knew and didn't love.

Well, she knew him. Love wasn't an option. The only

woman to own his heart had been taken from him. Now, he didn't have one to give. Love… He'd been down that road before and it was pitted with heartbreak, pain and loss. But Reagan wouldn't expect that from him. They had a friendship. And that was a solid foundation that a good many marriages lacked.

The idea—it was crazy. It bordered on rash. And his family would probably call it another one of his hare-brained adventures.

None of them understood why he pursued those exploits. He'd been in control of precious little in his life. Not his parents' untimely demise. Not where he and Luke landed afterward. Not Melissa's death. And even though he enjoyed his job at Wingate Enterprises, that family loyalty, the debt he felt he owed Ava and Trent, had compelled him to enter into the family business.

And now he had to bear witness to the slow crumbling of that business.

He didn't need a psychologist to explain to him why he had control issues. He got it.

When he climbed a mountain or dived from a plane, his safety and success were in his own hands. It all depended on his skill, his preparation and will. He determined his fate.

And while his chaotic and uncertain life was beyond his power, he could help Reagan wrest control of hers. As he remembered the girl who had stood with him during one of his loneliest and most desolate moments, it was the least he could do to repay her kindness.

Yes, it could work.

He just had to get Reagan to agree with him first.

Four

It'd been some years since Reagan had been to the Wingate estate.

Five to be exact.

The gorgeous rolling hills and the large mansion sitting on the highest point brought back so many memories of a happier, much less complicated time.

Though Reagan was a couple of years older, she'd been good friends with Harley Wingate when they'd been younger. Some would say the best of friends, who stayed in each other's homes, wrote in diaries and then shared their secrets and gossiped about boys. Reagan smiled, wistful. Those had definitely been simpler times.

Before her miscarriage and Harley leaving the United States for Thailand. Reagan had never revealed her pregnancy to her friend, and then Harley had left with her own secrets—including who had fathered her own baby.

Sadness whispered through Reagan as she drove past the home where she'd spent so many hours. A mix of Southwestern and California ranch architectural style, it boasted cream stone and stucco with a clay tile roof and a wraparound porch that reached across the entire second story. Memory filled in the rest. Wide spacious rooms, a library and dining areas, an outdoor kitchen that was a throwback to the ranch it resembled. Several porches and patios stretched out from the main structure and a gorgeous pool that she and Harley used to while away hours beside. Expensive, tasteful and luxurious. That summed up the home and, in many ways, the family.

Reagan's father had been proud his daughter was friends with a Wingate daughter.

She'd ruined that pride.

Not going there today. Not when she'd received a mysterious and, she freely admitted, enticing voice mail from Ezekiel Holloway asking her to meet him at the guesthouse on the estate. What could he possibly have to discuss with her? Why couldn't they have met at his office in the Wingate Enterprises building just outside of Royal?

And why had her belly performed a triple-double that would've had Simone Biles envious just hearing that deep, silk-over-gravel voice?

She shook her head, as if the action could somehow mitigate the utter foolishness of any part of her flipping and tumbling over Ezekiel. If the other reasons why he was off-limits—playboy, friend-zoned, he'd seen her with braces and acne—didn't exist, there remained the fact that he clearly still pined over his dead fiancée.

Eight years.

God, what must it be like to love someone like that? In her teenage folly, she'd believed she and Gavin had shared that kind of commitment and depth of feeling. Since he'd ghosted her right after the miscarriage, obviously not. And her heart had been broken, but she'd recovered. The scarred-over wound of losing her unborn child ached more than the one for Gavin.

Unlike Ezekiel.

It'd been a couple of days since she'd walked out of the cemetery leaving him behind, but she could still recall the solemn, grim slash of his full mouth. The darkness in his eyes. The stark lines of his face. No, he'd *loved* Melissa. And Reagan pitied the woman who would one day come along and try to compete for a heart that had been buried in a sun-dappled grave almost a decade ago.

Pulling up behind a sleek, black Jaguar XJ, Reagan shut off the engine and climbed from her own dark gray Lexus. Like a magnet, she glided toward the beautiful machine. Her fingers hovered above the gleaming aluminum and chrome, hesitant to touch and leave prints. Still those same fingertips itched to stroke and more. Grip the steering wheel and command the power under the hood.

"Am I going to need to get you and my car a room?"

So busted. Reagan winced, glancing toward the porch where Ezekiel leaned a shoulder against one of the columns. Unless he lounged around the house in business clothes, he must've left the office to meet her here. A white dress shirt lovingly slid over his broad shoulders, muscular chest and flat abdomen, while dark gray slacks emphasized his trim waist and long, powerful legs.

"You might," she said, heading toward him but jerking her all-too-fascinated gaze away to give the Jaguar one last covetous glance. "V8 engine?"

He nodded. "And supercharged." She groaned, and he broke out into a wide grin. "I didn't know you were into cars," he remarked, straightening as she approached.

Reagan climbed the stairs to the porch, shrugging a shoulder. "My brother's fault. He started my obsession by sharing his Hot Wheels with me when we were kids, and it's been full-blown since then. We make at least two car shows a year together."

"What else are you hiding from me, Reagan?" Ezekiel murmured, those mesmerizing green eyes scanning her face.

Heat bloomed in her chest, searing a path up her throat, and dammit, into her face. Ducking her head to hide the telltale reaction to his incisive perusal, she huffed out a small laugh. "Hiding? Please. Nothing that dramatic. I'm an open book."

He didn't reply, and unable to help herself, she lifted her head. Only to be ensnared by his gaze. Her breath stuttered, and for a slice of time, they stood there on the edge of his porch, staring. Drowning. At least on her part.

God. Did the man have to be so damn hot?

Objectively, she understood why so many women in Royal competed to have him in their arms, their beds. Even if it were just for hours. Oh yes, his reputation as a serial one-night monogamist was well-known. Was the rumor about him never actually sleeping with a woman true as well? Part of her wanted to know.

And the other?

Well, the other would rather not picture him tangled, sweaty and naked with another woman, period. Why just the thought had her stomach twisting, she'd rather not examine.

"C'mon in," he invited, turning and opening the screen door for her to enter his home.

Nodding, she slipped past him and stepped into the guesthouse he and his brother shared. *Guesthouse.* That brought an image of a garage apartment. Not this place. A towering two-story home with a tiled roof, wraparound porch, airy rooms with high ceilings and a rustic feel that managed to be welcoming, relaxing and expensive—it provided more than enough room for two bachelors.

It wasn't the first time she'd walked the wood floors here. After Luke and Ezekiel's parents died, they'd moved here, and she'd visited with Harley. But then, she hadn't been personally invited by Ezekiel. And they'd never been alone.

Like now.

"I have to admit, I've been dying to find out what all the cloak-and-dagger mystery is about," she teased as he closed the front door behind them. "I've narrowed it down to plans for world domination or spoilers for the next superhero movie. Either way, I'm in."

A smile flashed across his face, elevating him from beautiful to breathtaking. *That's it*, she grumbled to herself, following him into the living room. She was only looking at his neck from now on. That face elicited silly and unrealistic thoughts. Like what would that lush, sensual mouth feel like against hers? Did he kiss a woman as if she were a sweet to be savored? Or a full-course meal to be devoured?

God, she had to stop this. The man might as well be her big brother. No, scratch that. There were moral and legal rules against lusting after your brother like she did Ezekiel. Still, it was all shades of inappropriate and wrong. Mainly because while she didn't see him as a sibling, he definitely viewed her as one.

The reminder snuffed out the embers of desire like a dousing of frigid water.

Ezekiel snorted, gesturing toward the couch. "As if I would ever share spoilers. Now world domination…" He shrugged a shoulder. "I can be persuaded."

"I'm not even touching that," she drawled. "But your questionable values don't deter my curiosity one bit." She lowered to one end of the sofa. "So dish."

Rather than taking a chair or joining her on the couch, Ezekiel sat on the mahogany coffee table in front of her. His white dress shirt stretched across the width of his broad shoulders as he leaned forward, propping his elbows on his muscular thighs. All the teasing light dimmed in his eyes as he met hers.

Unease slid inside her, setting beneath her breast-bone. Unease and a niggling worry.

"What's wrong?" she whispered. "What's hap-pened?"

Harley? Her parents? Something else with Wingate Enterprises? She, like everyone else in Royal—hell, the nation—had heard of the trouble at their jet manu-facturing plant. Unlike the gossip swirling around the Wingates proclaimed, she didn't believe the allegations of corruption. They didn't coincide with the people she'd known for years. And she absolutely didn't believe that Ezekiel would've gone along with something so nefarious. They might not have been close, but the boy and man she'd called a friend had a core of integrity and honesty in him that wouldn't have abided any fraudulence or deception. Especially any that could potentially cost people their lives.

"Reagan," he said, pausing for a long moment. A moment during which she braced herself. "Marry me."

The breath she'd been holding whooshed out of her. She blinked. Blinked again. Surely, he… No, he couldn't have possibly…

"E-excuse me?" she stuttered, shock slowing her mind and tongue.

"Marry me," he repeated, his jade gaze steady, his expression solemn. Determined. "Be my wife."

Oh God. His determination slowly thawed the ice that surprise had encased her in, permitting panic to creep through. He'd lost it. He'd finally cracked under the pressure from the trouble at Wingate. What other explanation could there be?

"Ezekiel…"

"I'm not crazy," he assured, apparently having developed the talent of reading minds. Or maybe he'd interpreted her half rising from the couch as a sign of her need to escape. He held out a hand, stalling the motion. "Reagan, hear me out. Please."

He sounded sane. Calm, even. But that meant nothing. The man had just proposed to her—if she could actually call his demand a proposal. Who just commanded a woman to marry him? As if she were chattel—hold up. Now *she* was the one losing *her* mind. Demand, ask, send a freaking telegram… Nothing could change the fact that she'd suddenly plummeted into an alternate universe where Ezekiel damn Wingate had ordered her to become his wife.

All manners flew out the window in extreme circumstances like this.

"What the hell, Zeke?" she breathed.

The man nodded, still cool. Still composed. "I understand your reaction. I do. But just let me explain. And if you say no and want to leave, I won't try to stop you. And no hard feelings, okay?" She couldn't force her lips to move, and he evidently took her silence as acquiescence. "I've been thinking about our conversation at the cemetery for the last couple of days. Your situation with the will and not wanting to give in to your father's matchmaking campaign."

"Siege is more like it," she grumbled.

A corner of Ezekiel's mouth quirked. "Yes, we'll go with that. *Siege.*" Once more, his face grew serious, and she barely smothered the urge to wrap her arms around herself. To protect herself from the words to come out of his mouth. "The stipulation in your grandmother's will is you have to marry a suitable man in order to receive your inheritance. You also said you didn't want to marry a man you didn't know. A man who would try to control you." He released a rough, ragged breath. "We've been acquainted, been friends for years. And I have no interest in overseeing you or your money. As a matter of fact, I'm willing to sign a contract stating that your inheritance would remain in your name alone, without any interference from me."

"Wait, wait." She held up a hand, palm out, silently asking him to stop. To let his words sink in. To allow her the time to make sense of them. "Are you telling me you want to marry me just so I can access my grandmother's money?"

"Yes."

"But why?" she blurted out.

Unable to sit any longer, she shot to her feet and paced away from him. Away from the intensity he radiated that further scrambled her thoughts. Striding to the huge picture windows on one wall, she stared out, not really seeing the large stables or the horses in the corral in the distance. This time, she surrendered to the need to cross her arms over her chest. Not caring if the gesture betrayed her vulnerability, her confusion.

"Why?" she repeated, softer but no less bemused. In her experience, no one in this world did something for nothing. What did Ezekiel want from her? How did he benefit from this seemingly altruistic offer? "I've had no indication you were even interested in marriage." Only forty-eight hours earlier he'd been holding a vigil over the woman he'd wanted to pledge himself to for life. "Why would you voluntarily tie yourself to a woman you don't love?"

"I'm not looking for love, Reagan." She sensed his presence behind her at the same time his words reached her.

The quiet finality in that statement shouldn't have rocked through her like a quake, but it did. She wasn't looking either; that often deceptive emotion required too much from a person and gave too little back. But hearing him say it...

"I don't want it," he went on. "Love isn't included in the bargain, and you should know that upfront. Because if you need that from me, then I'll rescind the offer. I can't lie or mislead you. And I don't want to hurt you."

"I don't need it," she whispered. "But that still doesn't answer my question. Why?"

His sigh ruffled her hair, and as he shifted behind her, his chest brushed her shoulder blade. But rather than feel cornered or smothered, she had to battle the impulse to press back into him, to bask in the warmth and strength he emanated.

So she stiffened and leaned forward.

"Would it be advantageous for the world to believe that you, a member of the upright Sinclair family, are in my corner during this WinJet shit storm? Yes. Do I find the thought of companionship appealing? Yes. Is it hard admitting that not only am I sometimes lonely, but that it's an ache? Yes. They're all true, but not the biggest reasons for my proposition," he said.

Proposition, she noted, not proposal. Yet, she didn't latch onto that as much as him being lonely. God, she knew about the hole loneliness could carve. And how you might be willing to do anything to alleviate it.

"Freedom," he said. "That's what you whispered. Maybe you didn't mean for me to hear it, but I did. You long to be free. I don't know of what, and I won't pry and ask if you don't want to enlighten me. But it doesn't matter. I can give it to you. If you accept me, you'll have access to your inheritance and all those dreams and goals you mentioned won't remain stagnant for four more years."

She closed her eyes, a tremble working its way through her body before she could prevent it. He'd listened to her. That was a bit of a lark. Having someone pay attention, consider and not dismiss her needs, her desires. *Her.*

"I still don't think it's fair to expect you to legally

commit yourself to me. Marriage isn't something to be taken lightly," she maintained, although, dammit, her arguments against this idea were weaker.

"It won't be forever," he countered. "A year, eighteen months at the most. Just long enough for you to receive the money. Then we can obtain an amicable divorce and go our separate ways, back to being friends. Ray." He cupped her shoulders and gently but firmly turned her around to face him. He waited until she tipped her head back and met his unwavering but shadowed gaze. "Besides the obvious reasons, I understand why you might be hesitant to agree. I might be related to the Wingates, but with the fire and the bad press, our reputation isn't as clean as it used to be. And you might very well be dirtied by association—"

She cut him off with a slice of her hand between them. "As if I care about that," she scoffed. "No, my concern stems from this smacking of something out of an over-the-top TV drama. And that no one will believe it since we've never even been seen together as a couple. Or that all of this will seem like a stunt and only have more aspersions thrown your way."

"You let me worry about appearances and spinning this. I'm a VP of marketing, after all," he said, a vein of steel threading through his voice. "The only person we need to convince and impress is your father since he holds the reins to your inheritance. If he approves, we can have a quick wedding ceremony and start the ball rolling toward him releasing your money."

Reagan studied his beard-covered jaw. Jesus, she was really considering this propo—no, *proposition*. This was more akin to a business arrangement. Complete with a contract. Except with a ring. And a wedding.

And a commitment. A commitment without…

She lifted her gaze to his and found herself locked in his almost too intense stare. Which was going to make this all the more difficult to vocalize.

"I know you, uh…" Fire blazed up her neck and poured into her face, and she briefly squeezed her eyes shut. "I know you enjoy female company. Won't marrying me, um, interfere with…" She trailed off.

"Are you trying to ask me if I'm going to be able to endure going without sex?" he asked bluntly.

Damn. "Yes," she pushed forward. Because although she threatened to be consumed in mortification, she needed this point to be clear. "If I agree to this—and that's a big *if*—we have to appear as if we're in love even though it's not true. And that includes not going out on," she paused, "*dates* with other women while we're married."

She didn't even consider suggesting sex as part of their bargain. Ezekiel saw her as his cousin's best friend, not a desirable woman. Offering him the option would only embarrass both of them, and she'd tasted rejection and humiliation enough to last her a lifetime. There were only so many times a woman could be told she was unwanted in words and action before she sympathized with the turtle, afraid to stick out her head from her shell in fear of it being lobbed off.

"Ray, look at me." She did as he demanded, a little surprised to realize her gaze had dipped to his chin again. "I control my dick, not the other way around."

Oookay. Hearing him utter *that* shouldn't have been sexy. It should've offended her. But it was, and it didn't. If the flesh between her legs had a vote, she should have a mix tape made with him saying dick over and over again.

Proposition. Platonic. Friend. No sex.

She wasn't sure, but her vagina might have whispered, *Spoilsport.*

"I'm taking that as a yes, that other women would be out of the picture for the duration of our...arrangement," she said, arching an eyebrow.

"Yes, Ray." A smile curved his mouth, and she cursed herself for again wondering how he would feel, taste. Good thing sex was off the table. She probably wouldn't survive it with this man. "Now, your answer. Or do you need more time to consider it? Will you be my trust fund fiancée?"

In spite of the thoughts whirling through her head, she almost smiled at his phrasing. Did she need more time? His arguments were solid. His reasons for sacrificing himself to her cause still remained nebulous, but if he was willing...

She allowed herself to imagine a future where she was independent. Where her work at the girls' home in Colonial County would no longer have to be a secret she kept to herself out of fear of hurting her parents. A future where she could build a similar home here in Royal that supported teenage pregnant mothers who didn't have the family support, health care or resources they so desperately needed.

She should know. She had been one.

And this would solve her dilemma with honoring her grandmother's request even if the stipulation continued to hurt Reagan. She feared estrangement from her father, her family, and marrying Ezekiel would prevent that as well. Once, her father had been delighted about her friendship with a Wingate. Now she had the opportunity to marry into the family. Maybe he might even be…proud of her again?

Blowing out a breath, she pinched the bridge of her nose. Then lowered her arm and opened her eyes to meet the pale green scrutiny that managed to see too much and conceal even more.

"Yes, I'll marry you."

Five

"Are you sure about this?" Reagan questioned Ezekiel for, oh, probably the seventeenth time since she'd agreed to his...bargain. "It's not too late to back out," she said as he cut the engine in his car. Even riding in the Jaguar hadn't been able to banish the nerves tightening inside her. Which was a shame. The car rode and handled like a dream.

Long, elegant fingers wrapped around the fist she clenched in her lap, gently squeezing. He didn't speak until she tugged her scrutiny from their joined hands to his face.

"I'm sure, Reagan. Just like I was sure the last time you asked. And the time before that. And the time before that." Chuckling, he gave her hand one last squeeze before releasing her and popping open his car door. In seconds, he'd rounded the hood and had her own door open. He extended a hand toward her, and with a resigned sigh, she covered his palm with hers.

And ignored the sizzle that crackled from their clasped hands, up her arm and traveled down to tingle in her breasts. She'd better get used to doing nothing about her reaction to him. It was inconvenient and irritating.

Not to mention unwelcome.

He kept their hands clasped together as they walked up the steps to her home. Ezekiel had advised that they shouldn't waste any time getting the ball rolling on their plan. So she'd called the administrator of the girls' home and let them know she wouldn't be in today. Though she hated missing even one shift, Reagan agreed with Ezekiel. The sooner the hard part of telling her family was over with, the better.

Next, she'd called her parents to ensure they would both be home this evening for an announcement. Forcing a cheer she didn't feel into her voice as she talked to her mother had careened too close to lying for Reagan's comfort, and even now, her belly dipped, hollowed out by the upcoming deception. Necessary, but still, a deception all the same.

"Sweetheart, look at me."

Reagan halted on the top step, her chest rising and falling on abrupt, serrated breaths. But she tipped her head back, obeying Ezekiel's soft demand.

She didn't flinch as he cupped her jaw. And she forced herself not to lean into his touch like a frostbite victim seeking warmth. His thumb swept over her cheek, and she locked down the sigh that crept up her throat.

"Everything's going to be fine, Reagan," he assured

her, that thumb grazing the corner of her mouth. "I'll be right by your side, and I promise not to leave you hanging."

She just managed not to snap, *Don't make promises you can't keep*, trapping the sharp words behind her clenched teeth. Of course he would leave. Whether it was at the end of this evening if it didn't go well or at the termination of their "marriage." All men left, at some point. Gavin had. The affectionate, warm father she remembered from her childhood had, replaced by a colder, less forgiving and intolerant version.

As long as she remembered that and shielded herself against it, she wouldn't be hurt when Ezekiel eventually disappeared from her life.

"We should go in. They're expecting us." Stepping back and away from his touch, she strode toward the front door of her family home. A moment later, the solid, heated pressure of his big hand settled on the small of her back. "So it begins."

"Did you just quote *Lord of the Rings*?" he asked, arching a dark brow. Amusement glinted in pale green eyes.

"The fact that you know I did means we might actually be able to pull this 'soul mate' thing off," she shot back.

He gave an exaggerated gasp. "What kind of animal doesn't know Tolkien?"

"Exactly."

They were grinning at each other when the front door opened, and her father appeared in the entrance.

"Reagan." He paused, studying Ezekiel, his scrutiny inscrutable. "Ezekiel." He stretched a hand toward him. "This is a nice surprise."

As the two men shook hands and greeted one another, Reagan inhaled a slow, deep breath. *I can do this. I have to do this.*

Because the alternatives—a parade of men, more disappointment as she turned them down, trapping her in this half life—were hard for her to stomach.

"Well, come on in. We've held up dinner to wait on you." Her father shifted backward and waved them inside. "I'll have Marina add an extra setting for our guest."

"Thank you, Douglas. I appreciate you accommodating me on such short notice," Ezekiel said, his hand never leaving Reagan's back, his big frame a reassuring presence at her side.

"Of course."

Douglas led the way to the smaller living room where her mother waited. As soon as they entered, she rose from the chair flanking the large fireplace. At fifty-five, Henrietta Sinclair possessed an elegance and beauty that defied time. Short, dark hair that held a sweep of gray down the side framed her lovely face in a classic bob. Petite and slender, she might appear on the fragile side, but to play mediator and peacemaker between Reagan and her father for all these years, she contained a quiet strength that was often underrated. Admittedly, by Reagan herself.

"Well, you said you had a surprise, and this is definitely one," Henrietta said, crossing the room toward them. "Welcome, Ezekiel." She held both her arms out toward him, clasping his hands in hers. He lowered his head and kissed each cheek. "It's so good to see you."

"You, too, Ms. Henrietta," Ezekiel said. "Thank you for having me here." He gently extricated his hands from hers and returned one back to the base of Reagan's spine.

And her mother's shrewd gaze didn't miss it.

"None of this 'Ms. Henrietta' stuff. Please, just Henrietta," she admonished with a smile. "And you look beautiful this evening, Reagan." She scanned her daughter's purple sheath dress and the nude heels. "Any special reason?"

"Very subtle, Mom," Reagan drawled, shaking her head. Relief tiptoed inside her chest, easing some of the anxiety that had resided there since she and Ezekiel had left his home. Maybe this wouldn't be as difficult as she'd imagined. "Actually, Zeke and I would like to talk with you and Dad before dinner."

Her father moved to stand beside her mother, and his impenetrable expression would've made the Sphinx cry in envy. Reagan's nerves returned in a flood, streaming through her so they drowned out the words that hovered on her tongue.

Jesus, she was a grown woman. Why did her father's approval still mean so much to her?

Because it's been so long since you experienced it.

So true. In ten years, she'd tasted disappointment, glimpsed censure, felt his frustration. But it'd been so very long since his eyes had lit up with pride. A part of her—that sixteen-year-old who'd once been a daddy's girl—still hungered for it.

Maybe Ezekiel sensed the torrent of emotion swirling inside her. Or maybe he was just a supreme actor. Either way, he shifted his hand from her back and wrapped an arm around her shoulders, gently pulling her farther into his side, tucking her against his larger frame. Like a shelter.

One she accepted.

If only for a few moments.

"Douglas, Henrietta, as you know, Reagan and I have been friends for years. Since we were younger," Ezekiel said, his deep voice vibrating through her, setting off sparks that were wholly inappropriate. "In the last couple of months, we've rekindled that friendship and have become even closer. I've spoken to her, because it is ultimately her decision, but I also wanted to obtain your blessing to marry your daughter."

Silence reigned in the room, deafening and thick. Reagan forced herself not to fidget under the weight of her father's stare and her mother's wide-eyed astonishment.

"Well, I—" Henrietta glanced from the both of them to her father, then back to them. "I have to admit, I was expecting you to tell us you two were dating, not..." She trailed off. Blinked.

"I know it seems quick, Mom," Reagan said, stunned at the evenness of her tone. When inside her chest twisted a jumble of emotion—trepidation, fear...uncertainty. "But considering how long Zeke and I have known each other, not really. We just fell for one another, and it felt right."

Good God, how the lies just rolled off her tongue. She was going to hell with a scarlet *L* for *Liar* emblazoned across her breasts.

"Is that so?" her father asked, finally speaking. "Then why is this the first time we've heard of this... *relationship*?"

Reagan hiked her chin up, straightening her shoulders and shifting out from under Ezekiel's arm to meet her father's narrowed gaze. This was their vicious cycle.

His censure. Her hurt. Her defiance. Next, their mother would step in to soothe and arbitrate.

"Because we decided to keep it to ourselves until we were ready to share our personal business with everyone else. The only thing faster than Royal's gossip grapevine is the speed of light. We wanted to make sure what we had was solid and real before opening ourselves up for the scrutiny that comes from just being a member of the Wingate family and a Sinclair. There's nothing wrong with that."

"Speaking of that," Douglas added, his attention swinging to Ezekiel. His expression hardened. "With all that Wingate Enterprises is embroiled in right now, you didn't consider how that might affect Reagan?"

"Dad—"

"Of course I did, Douglas," Ezekiel cut in, his tone like flint. "I would never want to expose her to any backlash or disrespect. Believe me, I've suffered enough, and I don't want to subject her to that. Protecting her is my priority. But if my own past and this situation has taught me anything, it's that life is too short and love too precious to allow things such as opinions and unfavorable press to determine how we live. Then there's the fact that we are innocent, even if the court of public opinion has judged us. Family, our true friends and members of the Cattleman's Club believe in and support us. And they will support and protect Reagan as well. As a member yourself, you understand the power and strength of that influence."

Her father didn't immediately reply, but he continued to silently study Ezekiel.

"And I believe the Wingates are innocent as well, Dad," Reagan said. "We've known them for years, and they've always proven themselves to be upstanding, good people. The incidents of the last few weeks shouldn't change that." She inhaled a breath, reaching for Ezekiel's hand, but before she could wrap her fingers around his, he was already entwining them together. "*He's* a good man. An honorable one. I wouldn't choose a man who didn't deserve my heart and your trust."

As soon as the words left her mouth, she flinched. Wished she could snatch them back. But they were already out there, and from the twist of her father's lips, and the lowering of her mother's lashes, hiding her gaze, she could read their thoughts.

The last one you chose was a real winner, wasn't he? Got you pregnant, then abandoned you.

We don't trust your judgment, much less your capability of picking a worthy man.

Fury flared bright and hot inside her. And underneath? Underneath lurked the aged but still pulsing wounds of hurt and humiliation. *I'm not that girl anymore. When will you stop penalizing me for my mistakes? When will you love me again?*

"And this sudden decision to marry wouldn't have anything to do with your grandmother's will?" her father retorted with a bite of sarcasm.

Hypocrite. Her fingers involuntarily tightened around Ezekiel's. How did he dare to ask her that when he'd been throwing random man after man in front of her to marry her off? The only difference now was that she'd found Ezekiel instead of her father cherry-picking him.

"Dad, I don't need—"

"Excuse me, Douglas," Ezekiel interjected, his grip on her gentle but firm. "I'm sure I don't have to tell you about your daughter. She's not just beautiful, but kind, selfless, sensitive, whip smart, so sensitive that at times I want to wrap her up and hide her away so more unscrupulous people can't take advantage of her tender heart. That's who I want to be for her. A protector. Her champion. *And* her husband."

It's fake. It's all for the pretense, she reminded herself as she stared up at Ezekiel, blinking. And yet…no one had ever spoken up for her, much less about her, so eloquently and beautifully. In this small instant, she almost believed him.

Almost believed those things of herself.

"I don't appreciate you cutting me off, but for that, I'll make an exception and like it," she whispered.

Again, that half smile lifted a corner of his mouth, and when he shifted that gaze down to her, she tingled. Her skin. The blood in her veins.

The sex between her legs.

No. *Nononono.* Her brain sent a Mayday signal to her flesh.

"I don't know if I deserve Reagan, but I will do everything in my power to try," Ezekiel said, squeezing her fingers.

Affection brightened his eyes, and it wasn't feigned for her parents' benefit; she knew that. He *did* like her. "I know you have doubts, and I can't blame you for them. But not about how I will care for your daughter."

Her father stared at Ezekiel in silence, and he met Douglas's stare without flinching or lowering his gaze. Not many men could do that. And she caught the glint of begrudging respect in her father's eyes.

"You have our blessing," Douglas finally said. He extended his hand toward Ezekiel.

And as the two men clasped hands, her mother beamed.

"Well, thank God that's out of the way. Goodness, Douglas, that was so dramatic," Henrietta tsked, moving forward to envelop Reagan in her arms. The familiar scent of Yves Saint Laurent Black Opium embraced her as well, and for a moment, Reagan closed her eyes and breathed in the hints of vanilla, jasmine and orange blossom. Pulling back, Henrietta smiled at Reagan. "Congratulations, honey."

"Thanks, Mom," she murmured, guilt a hard kernel lodged behind her breastbone.

"Have you two thought about a date yet?" her mother asked, and Reagan swore she could glimpse the swirl of wedding dresses, flowers and invitations floating above her head. "What about next spring? The clubhouse is usually reserved months in advance, but your father has donated enough money to this community that they would definitely fit you in. And we should probably send invitations out now…"

"Mom." Reagan gently interrupted her mother's full steam ahead plans with a glance at Ezekiel. "We were actually thinking of just a small affair in a couple of weeks."

"What?" Henrietta gasped, and her horrified expression might have been comical under different circumstances. "No, no, that just won't do. What would everyone say? Your sister had a big wedding, and so did your brother. So many people will want to attend, and they need advance notice. I won't have my daughter involved in some shotgun wedding as if she's—" Her voice snapped off like a broken twig, her eyes widen-

ing as suspicion and shock darkened them. "Reagan, are you... You can't be..."

"*No,*" Reagan breathed. "No, Mom, I'm not pregnant."

And as relief lightened Henrietta's eyes, anger washed through Reagan. Despair swept under it like an undertow. When would she stop being the sum of her mistakes with her parents?

"Well, then, what's the rush?" her father asked, his head tilting to the side, studying her. There was a shrewdness there that she refused to fidget under as if he'd just caught her sneaking in after curfew.

"We want to begin our lives together," she replied. "There's nothing wrong with that."

"A wedding in two weeks is...unseemly," her mother complained, shaking her head, her mouth pursed in a distasteful moue. "Six months. That's not too much time to ask. It's still short notice, but we can plan a beautiful winter wedding befitting my oldest daughter and have it right here on the estate. It'll be perfect." She clapped in delight.

God, this wasn't going how she'd expected at all. If it were up to Reagan, she would hightail it to the Royal courthouse, sign the marriage license and have a bored judge legally tie them together. It seemed more fitting to this situation. Definitely more honest.

Weddings with arches made of roses and the finest crystal and favors in the shapes of rings and a towering cake—those were for couples who were truly in love. Who looked forward to a life together filled with devotion, family and golden years together.

Weddings weren't for people who had based their temporary union on desperation, pity and money. Who looked forward to a year from now when they could be free of obligation and each other.

Besides, this wasn't fair to Ezekiel. He hadn't signed up for all of this. Hell, she wasn't even his wife yet, and her parents were acting like interfering in-laws. Waiting six months to marry would only extend their agreed-upon timeline. He'd only counted on auctioning away a year of his life, not a year and a half, possibly two.

She shook her head. No, she wouldn't do this to him. It was one thing to allow her parents to pressure her, but another to subject Ezekiel to it.

But before she could tell them that the modest, small ceremony was their final decision, Ezekiel released her hand and looped an arm around her waist, pressing a kiss to her temple. Her belly clenched. Hard. Just a simple touch of his lips and desire curled inside her, knotting into something needy, achy. Stunned by her body's reaction, she froze, a deer with its hoof suspended over the steel teeth of a trap.

"I don't want to rob Reagan of having this experience with you, so if it's okay with her, we can wait six months," Ezekiel said. "I don't want her to look back years from now and regret anything. Her wedding day should be special."

How many times could a woman be struck speechless in the matter of minutes? Countless, it seemed.

"Zeke," she finally murmured, tilting her head back. "You don't have to do that…"

"It's no trouble," he replied softly. "Not for you."

She heard his gentle assertion, but she read the truth in his eyes. *Don't rock the boat.* Don't cause—what had been his word?—trouble. *Go along to get along.* That had been her mantra since she was sixteen. While before it had worked for her, now? Now it felt...wrong.

"Stop worrying, sweetheart. It's fine. *I'm* fine." The low, barely-there whisper reached her ears, and with a jolt, she opened her eyes, only then realizing that she'd closed them.

She searched his face, seeking out any signs of his frustration, his disappointment, his *pity*. God, which would be more like a dagger sliding into her chest? Each would hurt for different reasons. No matter how many times she glimpsed them in her family's eyes, they still pierced her.

But only understanding gleamed in his gaze. Understanding and a resolve that both confused and assured her.

For now, she'd concentrate on the assurance. Because if she permitted herself to become any more curious about Ezekiel Holloway—or worse, give in to the urge to figure him out—she might never be able to back away from that crumbling, precarious ledge.

"Okay," she whispered back.

"Wonderful," her mother crowed with another delighted clap of her hands. "We'll start planning right away. And we'll start with a date. How about..."

Her mother continued chatting as they all headed toward the formal dining room for dinner, but Reagan only listened with half an ear.

Most of her focus centered on the palm settled at the base of her spine and currently burning a hole through her dress.

The rest of it? It'd been hijacked by all the thoughts

spinning through her head like a cyclone. And foremost in those thoughts loomed one prominent question…

What the hell have you just done?

Six

Ezekiel glanced at his dashboard as he shifted into Park.

9:21 p.m.

Late, but as he pushed open his car door and stepped out into Wingate Enterprises's parking lot, he knew Luke would still be in his office. Ever since the shit had hit the fan with the fire at WinJet, the resulting lawsuits, bad press and plunge in business, his older brother had been damn near killing himself to create new areas of investment, including new hotels and the best corporate jet. As vice president of new product development, he seemed to view saving the company and jobs of their over two hundred employees as his white whale.

Ezekiel worried about him.

Usually, the roles were reversed. When their parents died, Luke had been the one to look out for Ezekiel, to care for him even though he'd only been twenty-one and grieving himself. And when Ezekiel had lost Melissa, Luke hadn't left his side, even moving a small couch into his younger brother's room to make sure if Ezekiel needed him, Luke would be right there.

So yes, Ezekiel was used to being the one on the receiving end of the concern. But now, every time he passed by his brother's room at the house and his bed remained unslept in, that apprehension dug deeper, sprouting roots. Being a creative genius had its pros and cons. Luke could come up with amazing ideas and projects. But he could also become obsessive over them, everything else—including his welfare—relegated to the it'll-take-care-of-itself class.

Ezekiel trekked across the lot, approaching the six-story building that sat right outside of Royal in a large industrial park. The unassuming, almost bland exterior of the structure didn't scream family empire, but inside... He pulled free his wallet and waved his badge across the sensor beside the door, then entered. Inside, the modern, sleek and masterfully designed interior projected wealth, professionalism and power. Aunt Ava had chosen every painting, every piece of furniture and fixture herself. Anyone walking into this building could never doubt the success of those inside its glass walls.

Striding across the empty lobby, he took the elevator to the sixth floor. As soon as the doors slid open, he headed directly for his brother's office. Unsurprisingly, he noted that Kelly Prentiss, Luke's executive assistant of five years, sat at her desk, even at this late hour. Dedicated to his brother, she ensured he ate and took at least minimal care of himself when no one else could.

"Hey, Zeke," she greeted, smiling at him, warmth

brightening her green eyes. The redheaded beauty still looked composed and fresh as if it were after nine in the morning instead of at night. "You know where he's at." She nodded her head toward the partially closed door adjacent to her desk.

"How's he doing?" he murmured, aware his brother had the hearing of a bat and wouldn't appreciate them talking about him behind his back. But if he asked Luke the same question, the inevitable "Fine," would tell him exactly zero.

"He's..." She paused, narrowing her eyes in the direction of his office. "Luke. Still trying to shoulder all of this. But I'm watching over him. And I'll make sure he gets home tonight instead of pulling another all-nighter."

"Thanks, Kelly. I'm going in. If you hear yelling, just ignore it. That'll just be me, wrestling him to the floor and trying to knock some sense into him. Y'know, business as usual."

She laughed, turning back to her computer. "I hear nothing and know even less. I'm practicing my speech just in case I'm called as a witness for the defense."

He grinned and forged ahead into the lion's den.

Luke perched on the couch in the sitting area, papers strewn all over the glass table. A disposable coffee cup teetered too close to the edge, a takeout container next to it. He glanced up from his study of the documents long enough to pin Ezekiel with a glare.

"You have never, nor will you ever be able to take me," he grumbled.

Ezekiel snorted. They'd both wrestled in high school and college, and though it pained him to admit it, he'd never been able to pin his brother. Of course, Luke had been in the 182 weight class, and Ezekiel had been in 170. But Luke had never let him forget his undefeated status.

Ass.

"What are you doing here?" Luke muttered, his focus returning to the work spread out before him.

Knowing he possessed a short window before he lost his brother's attention completely, Ezekiel dropped to the armchair flanking the couch.

"Since going home and talking to you wasn't an option, I had to come here. I mean, telling your big brother you're getting married isn't something you should do over the phone."

Luke froze, his hand stilling over a paper. Slowly, his head lifted, and astonishment darkened his eyes, his usually intense expression blank. He didn't move except to blink. A couple of times.

Ezekiel should've felt even a sliver of satisfaction at shocking his brother—a remnant of the younger sibling syndrome. But only weariness slid through him, and he sank farther into the cushion, his legs sprawled out in front of him.

"What?" Luke finally blurted.

"I said, I'm getting married." Sighing, Ezekiel laced his fingers over his stomach. "It's a long story."

"Start at the beginning," Luke ordered. "And don't skip a damn thing."

Instead of bristling at the curt demand, Ezekiel sighed and filled his brother in on his very brief "courtship" of Reagan Sinclair. When he finished, ending with the tense dinner at his future in-laws' house, Luke just stared at him.

Jesus, what if he'd broken his brain with this too-unbelievable-for-a-TV-sitcom story?

"So, wait," Luke said, leaning back against the couch as if Ezekiel's tale had exhausted him. "You mean to tell me, you're willingly entering an arranged marriage—arranged by yourself, I might add—so a woman you barely know can receive her inheritance? And that woman happens to be the daughter of Douglas Stick Up His Ass Sinclair? My apologies for offending your future father-in-law, but not really, considering you're the one who gave him that particular moniker."

"Reagan is hardly a stranger. She and Harley are best friends—"

"How many years ago?" Luke interrupted.

"*And* we have always been acquainted," Ezekiel continued despite his brother's interruption.

"Right," Luke drawled, his shock having apparently faded as that familiar intensity entered his gaze again. "But there's 'hey, great to see you at this nice soiree' acquainted, and then there's 'hey, be my wife and let's get biblical' acquainted."

"First, *soiree*? How the fuck old are you? Eighty-three?" Ezekiel snorted. "And second, I don't plan on getting 'biblical' with her. This is a purely platonic arrangement. I'm helping her out."

Purely platonic arrangement. Even as he uttered the words, *liar* blared in his head like an indictment. Yes, he didn't plan on having a sexual relationship with Reagan. But the images of her that had tormented his nights—images of her under him, dark eyes glazed with passion, slim body arching into him, her breasts crushed to his chest, her legs spread wide for him as he sank into her over and over… None of those were platonic.

In his case, not only was the flesh weak, but the spirit was looking kind of shaky, too.

But he hadn't popped the question to land himself a convenient bed partner. When it came down to it, his dick didn't rule him. He could keep his hands—and everything-damn-else—to himself. Sex just muddied the already dirty waters.

Reagan had claimed to understand that he wasn't looking for love, couldn't give that to anyone else. But she couldn't. Not really. It wasn't as if he longed to climb into that grave with Melissa anymore; he didn't pine for her. But her death—it'd marked him in a way even his parents' hadn't. At some point all children have to face the inevitability of losing a parent. And they even think about how that time will be. His mom and dad's death had been devastating and painful, and to this day he mourned them. But he'd known it would come, just not so soon.

Losing a young woman who not only had her whole future ahead of her, but he'd imagined would be part of his future, had, in ways, been more tragic. More shattering. Because she shouldn't have died. According to statistics, she should've outlived him. But she hadn't. And part of her legacy had been a deeply embedded fear that nothing lasted forever. Anything important, anything he held onto too tightly could be ripped from him. Oh, there existed the possibility that it might not. But he'd played those odds once and his heart had been ripped out of his chest, and he didn't believe he would survive the pain. Not again.

Melissa had taught him that he was no longer a betting man.

So while Reagan might claim to understand why she shouldn't expect love and some happily-ever-after with him, sex would potentially change that. Women like her... She wouldn't be able to separate satisfying a base, raw need from a more emotional connection. And he loathed to hurt her, even unintentionally. Though he'd never caught wind of her being seriously involved with anyone, something in those soft brown eyes hinted that she'd experienced pain before. And he didn't want to add to it.

So for the length of their "marriage," his dick would remain on hiatus.

"And what do you get out of it?" Luke asked, dragging him from his thoughts and back into the present. "Other than canonization for sainthood?"

Ezekiel shrugged. "Companionship. The knowledge that I'm helping a woman I respect and like achieve her goals. Plus, you can't deny that news of a Wingate family engagement and wedding would definitely detract from the gossip and bad publicity surrounding us and the company at the moment. Who doesn't love a whirlwind romance, right?" He sighed, leaning forward and propping his elbows on his thighs. "I know this doesn't make sense—"

"No, to the contrary, it makes perfect sense," Luke cut him off. "At least to me. I'm just wondering if it isn't as clear to you."

Ezekiel frowned. "What the hell is that supposed to mean?"

Luke leaned forward, mimicking his pose. "It means

you couldn't save Melissa, so you're trying to rescue Reagan."

"That's bullshit," Ezekiel snapped, anger sparking hot and furious in his chest. "One has absolutely nothing to do with the other." He shot to his feet, agitated. Too fucking...exposed.

He paced away from his brother, stalking across the office to the windows that looked out over Royal. Seconds later, he retraced his path, halting in front of Luke, the coffee table separating them like a tumbleweed blowing across a dirt street. "You accuse me of having a savior complex, but I'm not the one who's basically moved into his office, assuming the responsibility of saving this company all on his own. Analyze yourself before you decide to play armchair psychiatrist with me."

The silence between them vibrated with tension and anger. *His* anger. Because instead of getting in Ezekiel's face and firing a response back at him, Luke reclined back against the couch and stretched an arm across the top of it.

"Hit a nerve, did I?" he murmured, arching an eyebrow.

"Shut the hell up," Ezekiel snapped.

That shit his brother had spouted wasn't true. After Melissa, Ezekiel went out of his way to avoid becoming deeply involved with people outside of his family. He wasn't arrogant enough to think he could rescue people like a superhero in a suit instead of in a cape and tights.

"Zeke." Luke's sigh reached him moments before he stood and circled the coffee table. "What you're doing for Reagan? It's a good thing. I didn't mean to imply it wasn't or that you shouldn't do it. I'm just...concerned."

He set a hand on Ezekiel's shoulder, forcing him to look into the face that was as familiar to him as his own. "I need you to be careful, okay? I don't want you to get hurt again."

Ezekiel shook his head. "This is more of a business arrangement than a relationship. We both understand that. You don't have to worry about me. Everything is going to be fine."

Luke nodded, but the skepticism darkening his eyes didn't dissipate. And for the moment, Ezekiel chose to ignore it. Just as he'd chosen to disregard the unexpected urge to protect Reagan from her father's censure tonight. To put her happiness before his own preferences when he'd agreed with her mother's wishes to extend their engagement from two weeks to six months.

Reagan had never come across as fragile to him; though slim and petite in stature, she possessed a confidence and self-assuredness that made her seem unbreakable…untouchable. But tonight? There'd been moments when he could've sworn her bones had been traded for glass. And he'd fought the insane urge to wrap her up and cushion her from the strange tension that had sprung up at moments between her and her parents.

Luke squeezed his shoulder. "Telling me not to worry is like telling the Cowboys not to pass Amari Cooper the football. Ain't going to happen."

Ezekiel snorted, and Luke returned to the couch and his spread of papers. Before he lost Luke's attention completely to work, Ezekiel followed and swept up the empty coffee cup and takeout container. He crossed the room and tossed them in the trash can.

"Thanks, Luke," he said, heading for the office door.

"For what?" his brother muttered absently.

"For being there."

Luke's head snapped up, his light brown eyes focused and sharp.

"Always."

He was right about that, Ezekiel mused, letting himself out and closing the door shut behind him. Through everything, Luke had always been there for him. Had never failed him.

Even when Ezekiel failed himself.

Seven

Reagan stepped off the elevator onto the executive floor of the Wingate Enterprises building. She barely noticed the tasteful, expensive furnishings or exquisite decor that prevented the office from feeling *corporate* but instead exuded welcome and competence.

She did notice the silence.

And not like the peaceful stillness of the cemetery where she and Ezekiel had encountered each other weeks ago.

No, tension reverberated in this quiet. It stretched so tight, screamed so loud she curled her fingers into her palms to prohibit her from reverting to her six-year-old self and slapping her hands over her ears.

She strode past the desks with people bent over them, hard at work, and the office doors shutting out the world. The anxiety that seemed to permeate the air like a rancid perfume twisted her stomach into knots.

She'd seen the news this morning. Had blankly stared at the screen as words like *DEA*, *drugs* and *smuggling* were thrown at her by solemn-faced news anchors who were unable to hide the inappropriate glee in their eyes over a juicy story. Her first thought had been to get to Ezekiel. To see if he was okay. To…*protect him.*

Reagan shook her head as she approached the circular, gleaming wood desk that sat outside his shut office doors. There was no protecting him or his family from this latest development in what had become a perpetual shit storm that circled the Wingate clan and their company. And he didn't need or want that from her anyway. No, she was here to make sure her friend/fiancé wasn't reeling.

Pausing in front of the desk, she met the curious gaze of the pretty woman behind it. Recognition dawned in her brown eyes seconds later, and she smiled.

"Good morning, Ms. Sinclair. How can I help you?"

Glancing down at the gold nameplate on the desk, Reagan returned the woman's smile. "I'm well, Ms. Reynolds. I don't have an appointment, but is Ezekiel free for a few minutes? I need to speak with him."

"Of course. I'm sure he would love a visit from his fiancée this morning. It also happens he's in between meetings, so it should be fine." She lifted the phone from its cradle and punched a button. "Mr. Holloway, Ms. Sinclair is here to see you." She paused. "I'll send her right in." Replacing the phone, she nodded. "He's waiting on you, and belated congratulations on your engagement."

"Thank you," Reagan murmured, heading for Ezekiel's office.

Would she ever get used to being called someone's fiancée? No, not someone. Ezekiel Holloway's. She doubted it. Three weeks had passed since they'd announced their intent to marry to her parents, and sometimes it still felt like a dream. Or a nightmare. There were days she couldn't decide which.

Even though he expected her, she still rapped the door, then turned the knob. She entered and scanned the office, finding Ezekiel perched behind his desk, dark brows furrowed as he studied the computer monitor in front of him. For a moment, she entertained spinning around and exiting as quickly—and impulsively—as she'd made the decision to come here.

But Ezekiel glanced up, and she halted midstep, her heels sinking into the plush carpet.

God, he looked…exhausted. His brown skin pulled taut over the sharp slashes of his cheekbones, lending his already angular face more severity. Stark lines only enhanced the almost decadent fullness of his mouth, and guilt coiled inside her for noticing. Faint, dark circles bruised the flesh under his eyes as if it'd been some time since the last time he and sleep had been acquainted.

The news about the DEA investigation had apparently dropped sometime yesterday even though she'd just seen it this morning. That had probably been the last time he'd visited a bed. Weariness dulled his usually bright green eyes, and her fingertips tingled with the need to cross the room, kneel beside him and stroke the tender skin under his eyes, to brush her lips across his eyelids. Anything to remove the worry, anger and fear from those mesmerizing depths.

Instead, she remained where she stood. First, Ezekiel wouldn't appreciate her noticing those emotions in his gaze—would most likely deny their existence. And second, that wasn't what they were to each other. Business partners and friends, yes. But lovers kissed and comforted each other to ease pain. And they were most definitely not, nor ever would be, lovers.

Still... God, she wanted to touch him.

Inhaling a deep breath and cursing the madness that had brought her here, she moved forward until reaching the visitor's chair in front of his desk. She didn't sit but curled her fingers around the back of it and studied him some more.

"You look terrible," she said without preamble. Blunt, but preferable to *do you need a hug?*

A faint smirk tilted the corner of his mouth before it disappeared. "Thank you for that. But I doubt you drove all the way out here just to critique my personal appearance. What's going on?"

"I—" Damn. Now that she was here, awkwardness coursed through her. She smothered a sigh. "I saw the news this morning. I wanted to make sure you were... okay."

"Am I okay?" he repeated, loosing a harsh bark of laughter. She tried not to flinch at the sound but didn't quite succeed. "Drugs were found at the WinJet plant. Now, on top of falsifying inspection reports and causing injury to our employees, we're being accused of drug trafficking. The DEA has been called in. And we're the subject of a drug smuggling investigation. No, Reagan, I'm far from *okay.*"

He shoved his chair back and shot to his feet.

"Dammit." He cupped the back of his neck, roughly massaging it. He stalked to the floor-to-ceiling window that offered a view of the Wingate Enterprises property and the town of Royal. It was picturesque, but she doubted he saw anything but his own demons. "I'm sorry," he rasped several seconds later. "I didn't mean to snap at you. It's been a rough couple of days."

"I can only imagine," she murmured. After a brief hesitation where she silently ordered herself to stay put, she disobeyed her better judgment and crossed the floor to stand next to him. "No, actually, I can't imagine. And I'm sorry. The last few weeks must have been hell for you and your family."

"The workers who were injured in the fire sued, and we decided to settle the lawsuit. Just when we believed the worst had started to blow over, *this* happens. I can't—" He broke off, his jaw clenching so hard, a muscle ticked along its hewn edge. "It's like we're cursed. Like one of those bedtime stories where the family lives this golden, blessed life and then an evil witch decides to strike them with trouble from every turn." Emitting another of those razor-sharp laughs, he shook his head. "Goddamn, now I'm talking in fairy tales."

Her chest squeezed so hard, she could barely push out a breath. Ezekiel's big frame nearly vibrated with the strength of his tightly leashed emotions. His frustration, his confusion, his…helplessness reached out to her, and she employed every ounce of self-control to stop herself from reaching back out in return.

"I'm sorry," he breathed, rubbing his palm down his face, the bristle of his trimmed beard scraping in the silence. "Thank you for coming by. That was sweet of you, and though I didn't act like it, I appreciate it."

"It's what friends do," she replied, reminding herself out loud why she couldn't touch him.

"And fiancées?" Ezekiel asked, a hint of teasing underneath the weariness in his voice.

"Of course," she added with a casual shrug of her shoulder. "A real one would offer sex to comfort you, but the way our arrangement is set up…" *Oh hell.* Had she really said that? She'd been joking, but… Oh. *Hell.* "I was just kidding…"

She trailed off as he stared at her, the fatigue in his green gaze momentarily replaced by an intensity that vaporized the air in her lungs. The tension in the room switched to a thickness that seemed close to suffocating. She should say something, try to explain again that she was kidding. But was she? If he asked her for it, would she give her body to him? Let him lose himself for just a little while with her?

No.

Yes.

Images crowded into her mind. Images of them. Of him surrounding her, his thick, muscled arms encircling her and grasping her close as his large body surged inside her. Her thighs trembled, and her suddenly aching sex clenched. Hard. She swallowed a gasp at the phantom sensation of being possessed by him, stretched by him. Branded by him.

"But you're not my real fiancée, are you, Ray?" he finally said, and if his tone sounded rougher, well, she ignored it. She had to.

"No," she whispered. "I'm not."

"Because we're friends and you don't want me like

that, right?" he asked, that dark gaze boring into her. As if he could see the truth behind her careful lies.

"Yes, we're friends," she agreed, raising a hand to her collarbone and rubbing the scar there through her thin blouse.

"And you don't think of me like that. Do you?" he pressed in that same deep, silken voice.

"No," she lied. Even as her subconscious shamed her for breaking a commandment.

He didn't say anything to that, but something inside her made her suspect he agreed with her subconscious. Did he *want* her to desire him? Or was he just making sure she understood where their boundary lines were drawn?

The latter. Definitely the latter.

"What's next for you? For Wingate Enterprises?" she asked, desperately turning the conversation back to the reason she'd come here.

He shifted his gaze from her and back to the window. "I don't know," he admitted on a gruff whisper. Again, he rubbed the nape of his neck. "Once the DEA gets involved that could mean anything. They could freeze our assets. Confiscate anything they believe is related to the accusations. Lock the doors of the building. Arrest anyone they consider involved... *Fuck*," he snarled. "How did we get here?"

"It's just been a couple of days, Zeke. They'll find out who planted the drugs, and Wingate will be cleared."

He shot her a sharp glance. *"Planted?"* he demanded. He shook his head. "You would be the first person who suggested they were, and that we're not responsible for smuggling or trafficking."

She sliced a hand through the air. "That's nonsense.

Your family would never be involved in something like that. There's an explanation, but you being a drug kingpin isn't it." She snorted. Because yes, the idea of it was just that ridiculous.

"God, Ray," he said. And for the first time, his chuckle wasn't a humorless, jagged thing that scraped her raw. "Thank you," he whispered. "Thank you for the first real laugh I've had in days." He lifted his arm, and it hovered between them for a couple of seconds before he brushed the backs of his fingers across her cheek. "Thank you for not turning and hightailing it at my bark and braving my bite."

"Yes, well, I don't appreciate being snapped at. But for that apology, I'll make an exception and like it," she mumbled, echoing the same thing she'd said to him at her parents' home.

He obviously remembered because he smiled. But then his hand dropped away, and he sobered. "Ray," he said, his voice lowering. "If you're having second thoughts about marrying me, I understand. You don't have to be afraid to tell me."

"What?" Surprise rocked through her, and she frowned. "Why would I have second thoughts?"

He sighed, and the exhaustion crept back into his face. "The terms of your grandmother's will state you need to marry a suitable man. And when your father gave us his blessing, he didn't know that my family would soon be accused of being a criminal enterprise. There's no way he can be pleased with this turn of events. Or with his daughter becoming involved with it merely by association."

"I'm not tainted by you, Zeke," she snapped, offended. And yes, her father could be old-fashioned and stuck in his ways, but even he drew the line at convicting a man until he'd been proven guilty. "And I resent the implication that my being connected to you would. I'll handle my father. I'm not calling off the engagement. Are you?"

He hesitated, that springtime gaze roaming her face as if searching for the truth behind her words. Finally, he said, "No, I'm not calling it off."

"Good," she said, tone brisk. "Now, I need you to do something for me." She didn't wait for his acquiescence but strode across the room and settled down on the chocolate leather couch in his sitting area. "Come here. Please," she belatedly tacked on.

He slowly walked toward her, his forehead creased in a frown. "What's going on? Why?"

She patted the cushion next to her. "I meant what I said," she said, plucking up one of the brown-and-red-patterned throw pillows and placing it on her lap. "You look terrible. Like you haven't slept. Or eaten. I can't do anything about the food part, but I can make you take a nap. Here." She tapped the pillow. "Just for a little while."

"Ray..." he protested, halting at the foot of the couch. "I'm not a kindergartner. I can't just take a time-out. I—"

"Will fall down in exhaustion if you don't take care of yourself. This situation is only going to get worse before it's cleared up. If you're not going to watch out for yourself, as your friend, I will. So get over here. Now." She injected a steely firmness into her tone that she didn't quite feel. And part of her burned with pent-up desire. But God, she couldn't touch him. Definitely couldn't sex the worry away. But she had to do something. Had to give him…something.

"Seriously, Ray. I have a ton of work to do and fires to put out. And, dammit, I feel ridiculous," he grumbled.

"Can you just shut up and humor me? I did abandon a beautification committee meeting and poked the wrath of Henrietta Sinclair to drive all the way over here and see you. The very least you can do is give me a couple of minutes," she insisted, throwing a glare in just for good measure so he knew she meant business.

"For God's sake…" he muttered, lowering to the couch and reclining back, setting his head on the pillow across her lap. "One day you're going to make an excellent mother, seeing how well you have the guilt trip down."

His words punched her in the chest, and she couldn't control the spasm that crossed her face. With his eyes closed and his arms crossed over his chest, he didn't glimpse it, and for that, she was grateful.

Reagan pushed through the hollowness his innocent words left behind and pressed her fingertips to his temples. Slowly, she massaged the tender areas, applying just enough pressure to soothe. Over the years, when her father had come home tense from a hard day at work, her mother had sat him down and done the same. And he would release a rumble of pleasure just as Ezekiel did.

Gradually, his big body relaxed, and his arms loosened, dropping to his sides. His beautiful lips parted on a heavy sigh, and he turned his head toward her. It didn't skip her attention, that if not for the pillow, his face would hover dangerously close to the part of her that harbored no confusion about what it wanted from this man.

Even now, tenderness mixed with longing. With a languorous desire that wound its way through her like her veins were tributaries for this need. His wind-and-earth scent drifted up to her, and she just gave up and soaked in it. Here, under the guise of friendship and offering the little bit of comfort she could allow and he would take, she could lower her self-imposed barriers and just…bask in him. Soon enough she would have to raise them again.

For both of their sakes.

"Ray?" came his drowsy mumble.

"Yes?"

His thick, black lashes lifted, and she stared down into his eyes.

"Thank you," he murmured.

"You already said that," she reminded him.

"I haven't thanked you for being my friend."

"Oh," she said. "You're welcome, Zeke."

And damn if that reality check didn't sting.

Eight

"I'd have to say your engagement party is a success," Luke observed.

Ezekiel had to agree. Tuxedoed and gowned guests crowded into the great room of the Texas Cattleman's Clubhouse. Their chatter and laughter filled the air, and yes, by all appearances, his and Reagan's engagement party was going off without a hitch.

When he'd asked his cousin Beth to help him organize the party three weeks ago, she'd taken over, arranging to have it in the clubhouse where several people in the family were members. Several years ago, the club had undergone a major renovation, and now it was lighter and airier with brighter colors, bigger windows and higher ceilings. Tonight, floor-to-ceiling French doors had been thrown open to the July night, and the warm, flower-scented air filtered into the room, making the already cavernous area seem larger.

Flowers, white, tiny fairy lights and even a beautiful arch decorated the space, and the dark wood floors seemed to gleam. Tall lamps had been placed on the patio beyond the French doors and more of the lights had been entwined around the columns and balustrades. Linen-covered tables, with elegant hurricane lamps and more flowers adorning them, dotted the room and bordered a wide area for dancing.

Everything was sophisticated, luxurious and gorgeous. His cousin had managed to pull off the impossible in a matter of weeks.

Yet, Ezekiel hadn't taken a single easy breath all evening. Like that other shoe just hovered above his head, ready to plunge into the room at any moment.

"Even Aunt Ava seems to be pleased with your choice of fiancée," Luke continued. "Considering her higher-than-God standards, that's a minor miracle."

Ezekiel snorted, sipping from his tumbler of whiskey. Luke wasn't wrong. His aunt might be a thin, somewhat fragile-looking woman, with her dark blond hair brushed with the lightest of gray, but one look into those shrewd gray-green eyes, and all thoughts of frailty vanished. She was a strong, driven woman who had been a wife, was a businesswoman and mother. And if you asked her children, they might tell you in that order. The death of Uncle Trent had been a severe blow to her. But she'd begun to return to her old, exacting, often domineering self just before the issues with WinJet hit.

"I'm glad she came tonight," Ezekiel said, studying his aunt and the man next to her. "I see she brought Keith."

"Since when is Keith Cooper going to let her go anywhere without him?" Luke muttered, the dislike Ezekiel harbored for the man evident in his brother's voice. "I swear, it would be almost laughable how obvious he is if it weren't so pathetic."

As his uncle's best friend, Keith Cooper had been in their lives for years. On the surface, the man with the thinning brown hair, dark eyes and athletic build that had softened from one too many bourbons was an affable, laid-back man with an easy laugh. Married and divorced three times and with no children, he'd adopted the Wingates as his family. Or rather he'd inserted himself into their family.

And maybe that was what rubbed Ezekiel the wrong way. Keith was always there. Like a snake. The big, toothy smile didn't hide how he watched Aunt Ava with an avarice that made Ezekiel's skin crawl. No, Keith hadn't done anything overt to earn his dislike, but Ezekiel didn't trust him.

Not at all.

"So you know, I have my speech prepared," Luke drawled, tugging Ezekiel's attention from his aunt.

He frowned. "What speech?"

"The best man's speech. Beth set aside a time for toasts after dinner. With everything that's going on, I figured you just hadn't gotten around to asking me yet." Luke slid him a sidelong glance. "But I knew you would ask so I came ready."

"Well, that was subtle as hell." Ezekiel laughed. "Of course you're my best man. Besides, Sebastian said no." At Luke's scowl, he barked out another laugh. "Kidding. Damn. I'm going to need to ask Kelly to schedule an enema to get that stick out of your ass."

"Hilarious. You're so fucking hilarious," Luke grumbled, but a grin tugged at the corner of his mouth. "It must be that pretty-boy face that Reagan is enamored with because it sure as hell isn't your sense of humor."

"Oh, I disagree. I'm quite fond of both," Reagan interjected, appearing at Ezekiel's side and sliding an arm around his waist.

She tipped her head so it rested on his shoulder, and the casual observer would believe this woman, with her radiant beauty and equally bright smile was blissfully in love. Hell, he almost believed it. But apparently one of Reagan's many talents included acting. She didn't flinch or stiffen when he stroked her arm or held her close to his side. Instead, she'd flirted with him, gifting him with affectionate glances and warm smiles.

Reagan was an enigma.

A gorgeous, sensual enigma that he wanted to cautiously step away from before the obsession of figuring out her many pieces consumed him.

The same woman who appeared to be the perfect daughter bravely entered into a business arrangement of a marriage so she could quietly defy her family and claim her own future. The same woman who lived her life on the center stage of Royal society, but whose eyes glimmered with sadness when she didn't think anyone noticed. The same woman who went rigid when he just brushed a tender caress over her cheek but invited him to lay his head in her lap to offer comfort.

Who was the real Reagan Sinclair? And why did desperation to discover the truth rip and claw at him?

This curiosity, this need to… To what? He knew what. And it—she—was forbidden to him.

Yet…when she'd drawn his head to her lap, had

rubbed his temples with such care, he'd inhaled her delicious, intoxicating scent. Had locked down every muscle in his body to prevent himself from tearing away that pillow and burying his face between her slim, toned thighs to find out if her delectable perfume would be more condensed there. He'd closed his eyes against staring at the beautiful, firm breasts that had thrust against her blouse, fearful of seeing her nipples bead under the white silk. If he had, he might not have been able to stop until he had them clasped between his teeth, tugging, pinching…

Jesus Christ.

He lifted the whiskey to his mouth once more and took a healthy sip. Even now, with her hip pressed to his thigh, he wanted to hike her in his arms and show her and everyone else in the room how well they would fit together.

In truth, Reagan deserved a man who could give her all of his heart. A man who didn't view love as a trap with razor-tipped jaws. A man who could offer her security and a name that was above reproach.

He wasn't that man.

And yet, here he stood beside her, claiming her in front of family, friends and all of Royal.

When had he become so fucking selfish?

Luke cleared his throat, his eyebrows arching high. Laughter lit his brown eyes. And something told Ezekiel that Luke's humor was at his expense.

"What?" He frowned.

"Your fiancée asked you a question. But you seemed so engrossed in your drink, I think you missed it," Luke drawled.

A growl rumbled at the back of Ezekiel's throat, but

he swallowed down the curse he itched to throw at his brother. He harbored zero doubts Luke at least had a clue where Ezekiel's thoughts had been.

"I'm sorry, sweetheart," Ezekiel apologized, glancing down at her. "What did you say?"

"I asked you to go ahead and confess the truth," she said, shooting him a chiding glance. "You hired a battalion of party planners to carry all of this off. And they worked all day and through the night like shoe-making elves."

He smiled, cocking his head to the side. "I help run a hugely successful, national conglomerate. You think I can't handle the planning and execution of one party?"

She mimicked his gesture, crossing her arms for good measure. His smile widened. Since that day in his office a couple of weeks ago, they'd become a little closer. Friendlier.

And that was both heaven and hell for him.

"Okay, fine. I begged my cousin Beth for help. She and Gracie Diaz attacked it with a competency that frankly scares the hell out of me. And all I had to promise in return was that you'd help with this year's TCC charity masquerade ball. See? I'm a problem solver."

"So in other words, you pimped me out for a party. You're lucky I'm marrying you," she muttered, but ruined her mock-annoyance with a soft chuckle. "With Dad being a TCC member, I've assisted with past charity balls, so I'd be happy to help."

"I'm glad to hear that," he drawled. "Especially since Beth told me if I don't learn to ask my future wife for her opinion instead of just arbitrarily volunteering her for things, I might need to start Googling for a large doghouse now."

"Beth always was brilliant." Reagan laughed. "Oh, I met your cousins Sebastian and Sutton. And I have no idea how you can tell them apart. They're identical twins, but wow."

"Oh I know. I've known them all my life, and it's sometimes still hard for me to tell them apart if I'm not looking close enough."

Luke snorted. "They used to get into all kinds of shi—I mean, trouble—when they were younger, playing tricks on people."

"I can only imagine. And it's okay, Luke." She grinned. "I've heard the word *shit* before. You won't offend my sensibilities."

Luke chuckled, holding his hands up in the age-old sign of surrender. "Yes, but even though my mother is no longer here, I think she would come down and smack the back of my head for saying it in front of you."

"He's not wrong," Ezekiel added with a laugh. Nina Holloway had been a stickler for manners. "As far as telling my cousins apart, Sebastian has a scar on his lower back from when we were kids. Whenever they tried to play jokes on us and switch places, I would always grab one of them and look for the scar. I wouldn't advise doing that here though."

"I'll save that for the wedding reception then," she promised, and both he and Luke chuckled. God, she was sweet. And in ways, too damn innocent for him. "Are you about ready to head into dinner?"

"Yes." Because this piece of theater allowed him to, he stroked a hand down her long, lustrous waves. Then because he'd already admitted his selfishness, he tangled his fingers in the thick strands and tipped her head back. He noted the flash of wariness in the chicory depths, but she didn't turn from him, didn't playfully admonish him and pull away.

Granting her time to do either, he lowered his head and brushed his lips across her forehead. And because the feel of her under his mouth proved to be more of a temptation than he could resist, he repeated the caress over the gentle slope of her nose. Her soft but swift intake of breath echoed between them. "Lead the way," he murmured.

Slowly, she nodded and as he loosened his hold on her hair, she stepped back. The smile she flashed him trembled before firming. An apology for crossing boundaries lurched to his tongue.

But then he caught the heat swirling beneath the shadows in her eyes seconds before her lashes lowered.

That unintended glimpse arrowed straight to his dick.

Now it was his control that he clenched instead of her hair.

And when she reached back and entwined his fingers with hers as they headed across the room, he clung to the reasons why he couldn't escort her out of this party to the nearest dark room and fuck her senseless.

"Can you believe their arrogance? Being investigated by the DEA and throwing this party as if nothing is happening. Their gall is astounding. Even for Wingates."

Ezekiel's steps faltered and he nearly stumbled as the not-nearly-so-low whispers reached his ears. In front of him, Reagan stopped, her slim shoulders stiffening.

But another ugly voice piped up just behind them.

A disgusted snort. "I wonder if drug money is paying for all of this. Or blood money, as I like to call it."

"Goddammit," Luke quietly spat beside him.

Rage, pain, powerlessness and shame. They eddied and churned inside him, whipping and stinging. A howl scraped at his throat, but he trapped it, unwilling to give anyone more to gossip and cackle over.

"If you'll excuse me for a moment," Reagan said, her voice hard in a way he'd never heard from her. Not until she firmly disentangled her hand from his did he realize how tightly he gripped her.

Unmoving, he and Luke watched as she turned and crossed the short distance to the two older women who had been maligning them. Reagan smiled at them, and as if they hadn't just been ripping his family apart with their tongues, they returned the warm gesture. Hooking her arms through theirs, she led them through the crowd and toward the great room exit. She tipped her head to the club's security who unobtrusively stood vigil at the door, and in moments, the two men escorted the women out.

Ezekiel gaped at her as she retraced her path toward him and Luke.

"Holy shit," Luke marveled. "That might've been the hottest thing I've ever witnessed in my life."

"Watch your mouth," Ezekiel muttered. "That's my future wife you're talking about." But damn if Luke wasn't right. That take-no-shit act had been hot.

"Now," Reagan said, returning to his side, "we were headed into dinner." She clasped his hand again and moved forward as if nothing had interrupted them.

"I need to know, darlin'," Luke said, falling into step on her other side. Whether Reagan was his fake fiancée or not, she'd won his brother's admiration and probably his loyalty with her actions tonight. "What did you say to them?"

"Oh, I just thanked them for coming to celebrate our upcoming nuptials. But that I refused to feed mouths that could congratulate us out of one side and denigrate us from the other. Then I wished them a good night and asked security to escort them out."

Luke threw back his head on a loud bark of laughter that drew several curious glances. "Remind me never to cross you, Reagan Sinclair."

Pride, fierce and bright, glowed within Ezekiel, and even if their relationship was only pretense, he was delighted he could claim this woman as his.

And that scared the hell out of him.

Nine

"Reagan, I need a word with you, please."

Reagan paused midstep as she crossed her home's foyer toward the staircase, glancing at her father, who stood in the entrance to the living room.

Checking her thin, gold watch, she frowned. Just five fifteen. Douglas Sinclair routinely didn't arrive home until almost six o'clock from his law office. Had he been waiting on her?

"Sure, Dad. But will this take long? I have plans for this evening."

She'd agreed to accompany Ezekiel to a dinner at his family's estate at six tonight. But she'd lost track of time at the girls' home and was now running late. That had been happening more and more lately as her responsibilities at the home had expanded from administrative to more interaction with the girls.

Ezekiel didn't seem to mind when she called to apologize or reschedule dates. She should've told him by now where she spent the majority of her time, because after the engagement party three weeks ago, they'd grown even more comfortable with each other. Yet that kernel of fear that he would dismiss her efforts—or maybe worse, ask why she volunteered there—prevented her from confiding in him. As it did from admitting the truth to her parents.

But he wasn't her father. So maybe she would tell him tonight after dinner. Not…everything. Still, she could share this. *Maybe.*

Her father didn't reply to her but turned and entered the living room, leaving her to follow. Her frown deepened. What was going on? Douglas's grim expression and the tensing of her stomach didn't bode well for this conversation.

"Sit, please," he said, waving toward the couch as he lowered to the adjacent chair.

Though she would've preferred to stand—easier to make a quick exit—she sank to the furniture. "What's wrong, Dad?"

He crossed one leg over the other and propped his elbows on the chair's arms, templing his fingers under his chin. That sense of foreboding increased. She and her siblings deemed this position his Thinking Man pose. Which usually meant he was about to lecture one of them or deliver an edict they probably wouldn't like.

"Reagan, I initially went along with this sudden relationship with Ezekiel Holloway and gave you my blessing for the engagement, but now I have concerns," her father said.

"About?" she pressed when he didn't immediately continue.

Her heart thudded against her chest, and she forced herself to remain composed. Douglas Sinclair despised theatrics. And the last thing she could afford was for him to accuse her of being too emotional to make an informed decision.

"The Wingate name used to be spotless and above reproach in not just Royal, but Texas. But now, with this scandal about dirty dealings at the jet plants, employee lawsuits and now drugs, for God's sake, I believe it's been dirtied beyond repair."

"Miles Wingate proved that the family wasn't responsible for the falsified inspection reports. Which makes me doubt everything else about the drugs," she argued. "You've known the Wingate family longer than I have, Dad. You have to know they couldn't be capable of trafficking or anything as reprehensible as that."

"I don't know anything of the sort," he disagreed. "People are not always who they appear to be. And while Trent Wingate might've been a trustworthy man, I cannot vouch for his family. Not personally." He lowered his arms and leaned forward, pinning her with a steady stare. "Besides, in the eyes of the public, they are guilty. Their reputation sullied. I don't believe it is wise to connect your name—or this family's name—with theirs at this time."

Her stomach bottomed out. She'd suspected this was where he'd been heading. But hearing him state it…

"James Harris, the president of the Cattleman's Club, as well as other TCC members all support the Wingates. They're not worried about their reputations being 'sullied,'" she said, imbuing her tone with her dislike over his elitist word choice. Hadn't she assured Ezekiel weeks ago that her father might be conservative but not arrogant or self-important? She shook her head.

"Maybe you're too blinded by your...*affection* for Ezekiel," Douglas continued. "But I think the right decision for not just you, but this family would be to break off this engagement. After all, how would it look if my firm was associated with people being investigated by the DEA for criminal behavior?" His mouth curled in distaste, eyes narrowing on her. "This doesn't only affect you. Your mother is also receiving the cold shoulder from some members of this community because her daughter is marrying into that family."

"That family?" she repeated, giving a short, harsh chuckle. Although she found nothing humorous about this conversation. "God, Dad, *that family* has been here in Royal for generations. They've done an immense amount of good for not just this community but outside the city with their philanthropic efforts. They're good people. And because of an accusation, of a rough period they're suffering through, you would abandon them?"

She huffed out a breath. "Before Ezekiel was my fiancé, he was my friend. Harley was my best friend. I refuse to just throw them away because people who indulge in rampant speculation rather than fact have nothing better to do than sit in judgment. I won't be one of them."

"You have no choice," he announced, tone flat and brooking no argument. "Your grandmother's will stipulates that you will receive your inheritance if you marry a suitable man. I determine the definition of suitable. And Ezekiel Holloway is not it. If you go through with this marriage, I won't release one penny to you until you're thirty. And don't try to convince me that the inheritance isn't the reason for this shotgun marriage. I went along with it at first, but no longer."

Fury blazed through her, and as she rose, her body trembled with it. Only respect bridled her tongue when she wanted to lash out at the father she loved. Since she didn't trust herself to speak, she pivoted and strode out of the room.

"You will end the engagement, Reagan," her father declared from behind her.

She didn't bother to turn around or glance over her shoulder at him as she pulled the front door open and walked out of her home.

Ezekiel buttoned the cuff of his shirt, frowning as he crossed the foyer of his guesthouse to answer the knock at the door. That had to be Reagan. He'd received her terse text about being on her way, but not only was she fifteen minutes early, they'd agreed yesterday that he was supposed to pick her up from her house. He hadn't needed to hear her voice to guess that something was wrong.

In seconds, he opened the door and his suspicions were confirmed. Though she was as lovely as ever in a pair of light green, wide-legged trousers and a white camisole, her customary smile didn't light up her face. Instead, her lush mouth formed a straight, serious line and shadows dimmed her pretty eyes. Unease slicked a path through him, and he stepped back, silently inviting her inside.

"What's wrong, Reagan?" he asked, closing the door behind her.

She whirled around, facing him, and thankfully

didn't make him wait. "My father ambushed me when I arrived home." Her lips twisted into a bitter smile. "He's rescinded his approval of our marriage. Apparently, it wouldn't be good for his reputation or business. *God*." She thrust her fingers through her dark waves and paced across the foyer, her strides fairly vibrating with her anger. Pausing in front of a painting depicting the Wingate estate, she stared at it for several long moments. But he doubted she was really seeing it. "I'm sorry, Zeke," she whispered. "I'm so angry. And ashamed."

"Ray, look at me," he quietly ordered. When she slowly spun around, he studied her gorgeous features, noting the conflict in her eyes, the sad downturn of her mouth. The slight slump of her shoulders. "Your father's not wrong."

Fire flashed in her gaze, replacing the distress. The breath snagged in his chest at the sight. Dammit, she was beautiful, and that passion only enhanced it.

Still… He couldn't blame Douglas. In the weeks since he'd visited the older man's home asking for his blessing, Wingate Enterprises had started to free-fall. In the wake of this latest scandal, stocks had plummeted, most of their jet contracts had been canceled and there had even been some boycotting of their hotels. They'd had to start laying off staff. With company assets frozen by the DEA, they couldn't even liquidate their holdings to plug up the worst of the bleeding.

So no, Douglas had the right to be concerned about his daughter marrying a man who might not even be able to provide for her. Whose name could bring her more harm than good.

"Of course he's wrong," she snapped. "And I would

never abandon you just because of gossip and innuendo. What kind of person would that make me? What kind of friend would that make me?"

A smart one. Instead of voicing that opinion, he slid his hands into the front pockets of his pants and murmured, "You never did tell me what you needed your inheritance for, Ray. To go to such extreme measures like agreeing to marry me, you must have a reason, a purpose for the money."

Her expression smoothed, becoming the loveliest of masks. "I already told you. I want my freedom."

"I remember," he agreed, moving closer to her and not stopping until they stood only bare inches apart. "But over the course of the weeks we've spent together, I've also come to know a woman who wouldn't allow something like money to keep her from grabbing that freedom. No, there's something else."

He paused, cocking his head to the side. "Do you think I haven't noticed that you disappear during the day several times a week? As much as I remember the girl you used to be, the woman is still sometimes a mystery. You're keeping secrets, Ray. And your reason for needing this money is one of them." He slid a hand free and pinched a lock of her hair between his thumb and finger, rubbing the rough silk of it. "You can trust me with your secrets, sweetheart."

Indecision flared in her eyes before her lashes lowered, hiding her emotion from him. But he caught the slight quiver of her lips before they firmed.

"Trust me," he damn near pleaded. His desperation for her to do just that shook him. But he didn't rescind the words.

The thick fringe of lashes lifted, and she stared at

"*4 for 4*" MINI-SURVEY

We are prepared to **REWARD** you with 4 FREE Books and Free Gifts for completing our MINI SURVEY!

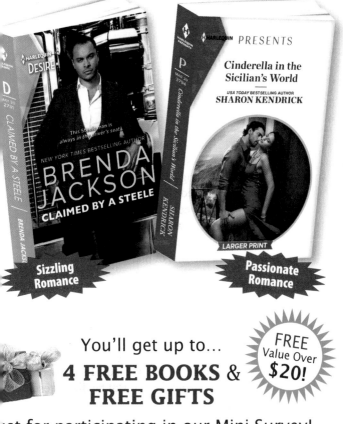

Sizzling Romance

Passionate Romance

You'll get up to...

4 FREE BOOKS & FREE GIFTS

FREE Value Over $20!

ust for participating in our Mini Survey!

Get Up To 4 Free Books!

Dear Reader,

IT'S A FACT: if you answer 4 quick questions, we'll send you 4 FREE REWARDS from each series you try!

Try **Harlequin® Desire** books featuring the worlds of the American elite with juicy plot twists, delicious sensuality and intriguing scandal.

Try **Harlequin Presents®** Larger-Print books featuring the glamourous lives of royals and billionaires in a world of exotic locations, where passion knows no bounds.

Or **TRY BOTH!**

I'm not kidding you. As a leading publisher of women's fiction, we value your opinions… and your time. That's why we are prepared to reward you handsomely for completing our mini-survey. In fact, we have 4 Free Rewards for you, including 2 free books and 2 free gifts from each series you try!

Thank you for participating in our survey,

Pam Powers

www.ReaderService.com

To get your 4 FREE REWARDS:
Complete the survey below and return the insert today to receive up to 4 FREE BOOKS and FREE GIFTS guaranteed!

◀ DETACH AND MAIL CARD TODAY! ▼

"*4 for 4*" MINI-SURVEY

1 Is reading one of your favorite hobbies?

YES NO

2 Do you prefer to read instead of watch TV?

YES NO

3 Do you read newspapers and magazines?

YES NO

4 Do you enjoy trying new book series with FREE BOOKS?

YES NO

Please send me my Free Rewards, consisting of **2 Free Books from each series I select** and **Free Mystery Gifts**. I understand that I am under no obligation to buy anything, as explained on the back of this card.

❑ **Harlequin Desire®** (225/326 HDL GQ3X)
❑ **Harlequin Presents® Larger-Print** (176/376 HDL GQ3X)
❑ **Try Both** (225/326 & 176/376 HDL GQ4A)

FIRST NAME	LAST NAME

ADDRESS

APT.#	CITY

STATE/PROV.	ZIP/POSTAL CODE

EMAIL ❑ Please check this box if you would like to receive newsletters and promotional emails from Harlequin Enterprises ULC and its affiliates. You can unsubscribe anytime.

Your Privacy – Your information is being collected by Harlequin Enterprises ULC, operating as Reader Service. For a complete summary of the information we collect, how we use this information and to whom it is disclosed, please visit our privacy notice located at https://corporate.harlequin.com/privacy-notice. From time to time we may also exchange your personal information with reputable third parties. If you wish to opt out of this sharing of your personal information, please visit www.readerservice.com/consumerschoice or call 1-800-873-8635. **Notice to California Residents** – Under California law, you have specific rights to control and access your data. For more information on these rights and how to exercise them, visit https://corporate.harlequin.com/california-privacy.

® and ™ are trademarks owned and used by the trademark owner and/or its licensee. Printed in the U.S.A.

HD/HP-520-MS20

HARLEQUIN READER SERVICE—Here's how it works:

Accepting your 2 free books and 2 free gifts (gifts valued at approximately $10.00 retail) places you under no obligation to buy anything. You may keep the books and gifts and return the shipping statement marked "cancel." If you do not cancel, approximately one month later we'll send you more books from the series you have chosen, and bill you at our low, subscribers-only discount price. Harlequin Presents® Larger-Print books consist of 6 books each month and cost $5.80 each in the U.S. or $5.99 each in Canada, a savings of at least 11% off the cover price. Harlequin Desire® books consist of 6 books each month and cost just $4.55 each in the U.S. or $5.24 each in Canada, a savings of at least 13% off the cover price. It's quite a bargain! Shipping and handling is just 50¢ per book in the U.S. and $1.25 per book in Canada*. You may return any shipment at our expense and cancel at any time — or you may continue to receive monthly shipments at our low, subscribers-only discount price plus shipping and handling. *Terms and prices subject to change without notice. Prices do not include sales taxes which will be charged (if applicable) based on your state or country of residence. Canadian residents will be charged applicable taxes. Offer not valid in Quebec. Books received may not be as shown. All orders subject to approval. Credit or debit balances in a customer's account(s) may be offset by any other outstanding balance owed by or to the customer. Please allow 3 to 4 weeks for delivery. Offer available while quantities last.

If offer card is missing write to: Harlequin Reader Service, P.O. Box 1341, Buffalo, NY 14240-8531 or visit www.ReaderService.com

BUSINESS REPLY MAIL
FIRST-CLASS MAIL   PERMIT NO. 717   BUFFALO, NY

POSTAGE WILL BE PAID BY ADDRESSEE

HARLEQUIN READER SERVICE
PO BOX 1341
BUFFALO NY 14240-8571

NO POSTAGE
NECESSARY
IF MAILED
IN THE
UNITED STATES

him. Weighing him. And relief flowed through Ezekiel when her lips parted because she'd obviously found him worthy.

"I plan to open a fully staffed and independent home for pregnant teen mothers here in Royal."

Shock quaked through him, pleasure rippling in its wake. Jesus. Of all the things he'd expected her to say, a haven for unwed mothers hadn't even been in the top ten. Admiration for her lit him up from within. Outside of his family, most of the socialites he knew served on boards or committees for charities, but very few desired to get their hands dirty.

Why *this* cause? Did she know someone who'd been pregnant, abandoned and homeless? The questions crowded onto his tongue, but rather than ask them, he cupped her face between his hands, stepping closer to her. "This is important to you, isn't it?"

Reagan nodded, and her lips parted as if to offer him an explanation, but after a hesitation, she closed them again, shifting her gaze over his shoulder.

"No, sweetheart, please don't look away from me." When she returned her regard to him, he swept his thumb over her cheek, and for a moment, he wished it was his mouth tracing the curve, tasting that soft, beautiful skin. "Thank you."

"For what?" she breathed.

"For trusting me with that information. I'm assuming your parents don't know about your plans?"

She shook her head, her hair caressing the backs of his hands and wrists. "No. They…wouldn't approve."

"Your secret is safe with me. And, Ray?" He settled a thumb under her chin, tilting her head back so she had no choice but to meet his gaze. His heart thumped against his sternum, and he viciously cursed himself for what he had to do. "Your project is also safe with me. Which is why I'm breaking off this engagement."

Hurt and anger flashed across her face. Her brows drew down into a frown as she settled her palms on his chest. She pushed at him, but he braced himself, refusing to be budged. Instead, he tightened his hold on her.

"Let me go, Ezekiel," she demanded. "If you don't want—"

"Want what, Ray?" he snarled. "Want you to have your freedom, your dreams sooner rather than four years from now? Want you to not damage your relationship with your family over me? Want you to have everything you deserve?" *Want you?* He ground his teeth together, trapping that last question. "I want all of that for you. And whether you admit it or not, your father, your mother—they're important to you. And I'm not going to let you risk that."

Not for me.

She sighed and the soft gust of air brushed over his skin. Like a kiss.

"It's not right. None of it," she whispered, the fingers that were trying to push him away seconds ago curling into his shirt. "I wish…"

Her voice trailed off, and he was grateful. Because a part of him hungered to know what she wished, what she desired. Maybe it was for the best—for both of them—that they were making a clean break. Before they crossed a line that neither of them could come back from.

That they would ultimately regret.

Giving in to a need that he refused to acknowledge, he lowered his head and pressed his mouth to her forehead. He inhaled her honeysuckle-and-cream scent, capturing it like a photograph. Her breath tickled his neck, and he stood still for a long moment, enjoying the sensation on his skin.

Lifting his head, he met her gaze. His gut tightened to the point of pain. Sadness swirled in those chicory depths. But so did a touch of heat, of desire. *Fuck.* It wouldn't require more than the barest of movements to take her mouth. To possess it. To find out if his dirtiest midnight fantasies about her texture, her taste came close to reality. With one tiny shift, he could satisfy his curiosity and just *know...*

He stepped back, dropping his arms to his sides. "You'd better go before your family starts to wonder where you are," he said, forcing a neutrality into his voice that didn't exist.

"Right," she agreed softly. "Take care of yourself, Zeke."

"You, too, Ray."

He turned to watch her leave, and though she paused on the threshold of the front entrance after opening the door, she didn't turn around or glance over her shoulder at him.

Only when she left and he stared at a closed door did he exhale and shut his eyes.

He should be grateful. Relieved. And he was. But damn if he could decide if he'd dodged a bullet or lost the one thing that had given him purpose these last few weeks.

Given him peace.

He shook his head and pivoted on his heel, heading for the staircase.

It didn't matter. She was gone.

And in the end, it was for the best.

For both of them.

Ten

Reagan stepped into the cool interior of the restaurant with a sigh, thankful to be out of the early September heat. It was only about three weeks from the official start of fall, but Texas didn't know it. Fixing a polite smile on her face, she strode to the maître d's stand.

"Hello," she greeted. "I'm meeting Douglas Sinclair. He should have already arrived."

"Of course," the young man said, nodding. "Please follow me."

She was ten minutes late for lunch with her father, but considering he'd sprung the "invitation" on her an hour ago, it couldn't be helped. He should be thankful she'd rearranged her plans to meet him anyway.

The only reason she had acquiesced to this impromptu lunch date was because he'd made it seem important, urgent even. It'd been two weeks since her father had demanded she end her engagement with Eze-kiel, and a part of her still resented him for that. But maybe this lunch could be the start of healing that rift. Her father loved her; in her heart, she acknowledged he only wanted the best for her. Even if he could be overbearing and stubborn, she'd never doubted that…

"Reagan." Douglas stood from a table next to the large picture window that looked over downtown Royal. "We've been waiting on you. You look lovely."

She barely registered the kiss he pressed to her hair, focusing on the *we*. This was supposed to be a lunch for just the two of them. But as her attention snagged on the man also rising from his chair, a cold sliver of hurt and anger settled between her ribs.

Of course her father hadn't just wanted to spend quality time with her. He had his own agenda, and that trumped everything.

"Reagan, I'd like to introduce you to Justin McCoy. Justin…" he smiled broadly at the other man "…my beautiful daughter Reagan Sinclair."

Justin McCoy. The tall, handsome man with light blond hair smiled at her, his blue eyes quickly roaming over her before meeting her gaze again.

God, she needed a shower. She cut her father a sharp side glance.

"It's an absolute pleasure to meet you, Reagan," Justin said, grasping her hand although she hadn't offered it. He lifted it toward his lips, and her stomach lurched. If not for her father's eagle-eyed gaze, she would've snatched her arm back. Especially since she hadn't given Justin permission to touch her.

On second thought…

She tugged her hand back before Justin could touch

her, ignoring her father's frown and Justin's shock. She didn't believe in the *ask forgiveness rather than permission* school of thought. And if neither this man nor her father respected her boundaries, then she didn't have to allow a man who was at best a gold digger to put his hands or mouth on her to spare their egos.

That simmering anger stirred to a boil, and she dragged in a breath before forcing a politeness to her tone that required Herculean effort on her part.

"Mr. McCoy, if you would excuse us for a moment. I need to have a quick, private word with my father."

Not waiting for either man's agreement, she whirled on the heel of her nude stiletto and stalked toward the exit. She pushed through the door and waited for her father on the sidewalk outside the restaurant.

She didn't have long to wait before he appeared.

"How dare you embarrass me like that, Reagan," he fumed, fury glittering in his narrowed glare. "You go back in there right now and apologize for your rude behavior."

"I will not."

His chin jerked up as if her words had delivered a physical slap, and his lips slackened. She'd shocked him. Hell, she'd shocked herself. Her heart drummed against her rib cage, and the tiniest sliver of fear slid through her veins. Since she'd returned to Royal and her family from that home without her baby, empty and ashamed, she hadn't once defied either of her parents. Especially her father. And she would be lying to herself if she didn't admit it scared her now. But no.

Just. No. Apparently, she had her limits, and she'd reached them.

"Reagan—"

"I'm not an idiot, Dad," she interrupted, slicing her hand through the air for emphasis. "I clearly see what this is. An ambush. Another setup. Well, I refuse to go along with it. Not this time. And definitely not with *him*."

"Yes, you will, Reagan," he hissed, his attention shooting over her shoulder. Most likely ensuring no one stood witness to her insolence, as he no doubt saw it. "I won't stand for this blatant disrespect. And I don't know what you think you know about Justin McCoy—"

"It isn't what I *think* I know," she shot back. "That man in there intentionally seduced an innocent girl and got her pregnant just so he could worm his way into a wealthy family. Considering our family history, you would think impregnating a girl would be at the top of your unworthy traits list," she sneered.

"Lower your voice this instant," he ordered, once more glancing around them. And that tore through her like a red-hot sword. Of course. They couldn't chance anyone overhearing about their shameful family secret. "Wasn't it you who told me I shouldn't listen to rumors and conjecture?"

"Rumors?" She released a jagged bark of laughter. "It's not an opinion that he used Julie Wheeler only to abandon her. It's not opinion that he tried to do the exact same thing with Beth Wingate. Ask Camden Guthrie or Bruce Wheeler. I promise you they will confirm that Justin McCoy's complete lack of a moral compass is a fact. After all, it was Cam's dead wife and Bruce's daughter he betrayed."

"It is my job as your father to decide what is best for

you, Reagan. And I might have failed once but never again," he ground out.

Had she thought he'd hurt her before? No, this… this was pain. Having him affirm that he believed he'd failed—that she'd been a failure.

Her breath shuddered out of her, and she blinked back the sting of hot tears.

She loved her father, but at this moment, he disappointed her just as she surely disappointed him. Douglas thought the purse strings controlled her, had kept her obedient and quiet for all these years. But he couldn't have been more wrong. Longing for his approval had. For her mother's, too, but more so his. There was no turning back the hands of time to that innocent period when she'd been a daddy's girl. She might never have what she desperately craved from him. The only difference between now and an hour ago was that she no longer cared.

"And the fact that you would believe he is a better man, a more *suitable* man than Ezekiel Holloway stuns and disheartens me." She shook her head. "I love you, Dad, but I'm not going along with this anymore. I know you want what's best for me, but you've never asked me what that is. You don't care. And that saddens me even more."

She turned and walked away from him. And even when he called her name, she didn't stop.

She was through answering to him.

From now on, she would only answer to herself.

"Mr. Holloway, Reagan Sinclair is here to see you."

Ezekiel jerked his head up from studying a report at his executive assistant's announcement through the telephone's intercom. Alarm blared inside him, and he shot up from his chair, already rounding the desk and stalking toward the office door. There had been no communication between them since he and Reagan had broken off their engagement. What had happened to make her end the radio silence now?

Before he reached the door, it swung open and Reagan stepped in. The impact of her after weeks of not seeing her halted him midstride. Jesus, had he really somehow forgotten how beautiful she was? Or had he just tried to convince himself she wasn't so he could stop thinking about her? Either way, the attempt had been an epic fail.

He'd missed everything about her—her laugh, her quiet way of listening, the cultured yet sensual husky tone of her voice, her scent…her friendship. And hell yes, he'd missed just looking at her. Today, her sleeveless wrap dress molded to her slim but curvaceous figure like a secret admirer, and damn him, but he was jealous of the material that cupped her lovely breasts, slid over the flare of her hips and glided down those slender, perfect thighs. His fingers itched to follow the same paths, to explore that uncharted territory for himself. And to stake his claim.

But she wasn't his anymore. Not even for pretend.

What had been unattainable before had become even more of an impossibility.

Forcing his unruly thoughts and wayward body under control, he demanded, "Reagan, what're you doing here?" The worry at the obvious distress in her eyes and the slightly jerky movement in her normally smooth gait roughened his voice. "What's wrong?"

"Marry me."

He stared at her, struck speechless. Dozens of questions bombarded him, and he mentally waded through them, finally settling on the most important one. "What?"

"Marry me," she repeated, closing the short distance between them, not stopping until her hands fisted the lapels of his suit jacket, her thighs braced against his and that honeysuckle scent embraced him like a long-lost lover.

He swallowed a groan at her nearness, at the feel of her body pressed to his. Lust, hot and hungry, punched him in the gut, then streamed through him in a swollen flood. Desperate to place distance between them so he could fucking *think*, he gripped her hips to set her away from him. But touching her backfired. Instead of pushing her back, he held her close, his body rebelling and taking control. Two weeks. It'd been two *long* weeks.

"Reagan," he rumbled.

"No, Zeke. Don't give me all the reasons why we shouldn't. I don't care. Do you know where I just came from?" she asked, switching topics with a lightning speed that left him floundering. Between that and his dick finding cushion against her stomach, he couldn't keep up. "I just left a restaurant where my father arranged for me to have lunch with Justin McCoy."

"The *hell*?" His grip on her tightened. Douglas had set her up with that asshole?

"Yes." Reagan nodded as if reading his mind. "Apparently my father considered him a more suitable match than you. A man who uses and throws away women for his own gain rather than you, a man who has been nothing but honorable and unfailingly kind and respectful. I had enough. I walked away from him and his machinations. I'm through allowing him to run my life, to make choices for me out of guilt and loyalty."

Guilt? What the hell did that mean?

Shoving the questions aside for the moment, he refocused on her. "I understand your anger, believe me, I do, but take a moment and think this through before you make a mistake you can't take back. This decision will cost you your inheritance. It could damage your relationship with your parents. Is this rebellion worth that? Because you're not in…" He couldn't finish that sentence. Couldn't fathom it.

"No, Zeke, I'm not in love with you," she assured him, and he exhaled a heavy breath. Even as an unidentifiable emotion twisted in his chest. "And maybe this is a little bit of rebellion on my part, but it's so much more. I'm taking control—of my choices, my mind, my life. I respect you, Zeke. But this isn't about you. It's about me. About finally becoming the woman I've been too afraid to own. So, from now on, I'm making my own decisions," she continued. "And that includes you. I choose you, Zeke. And I want you to marry me."

Jesus, did she know what a delicious temptation she was? How he'd fought following after her that evening he'd let her walk out of his house? That had required strength he hadn't realized he possessed. Doing it a second time…

No, she might feel certain here in this office, but she was still upset. Could feel very differently in the morning, hell, hours from now. Maybe after they talked this out, she would see—

She rose on her toes and crushed her mouth to his.

Oh fuck.

His control snapped.

Like a flash fire, the press of her lips to his poured gasoline over the lust that had been steadily simmering. He took possession of that sweet siren's mouth, claiming it with a thrust of his tongue. Possessing it with a long, wet lick. Corrupting it with an erotic tangle and suck that left little to the imagination about what he wanted from her.

And he wanted it all. In this moment where the lines between platonic friendship and desire incinerated beneath his greedy mouth and her needy whimpers, he wanted everything she had to give him.

With an almost feral growl, he reached between them and grasped her wrists, tugging her arms behind her. He cuffed them with one hand and thrust the other into her hair, fisting the strands and jerking her head back for a deeper, dirtier kiss even as he pressed her curves flush against him. Her breasts, so soft, so full, pillowed against his chest and her belly welcomed his erection. His legs bracketed hers, and he shamelessly used the position to grind against her, letting her know without any question how much she affected him. How hard she made him.

Though he dominated her body, she wasn't submissive to him. God no. Her mouth moved over his as if he were her first or last meal. Her teeth nipped at his lips, and he knew when this feasting ended, his lips would be as swollen as hers. She met him thrust for thrust, lick for lick, sweep for sweep. She was his equal.

No. He shuddered as she drew on his tongue, sucking. He was her supplicant. And he would do any goddamn thing for her as long as she didn't stop.

The loud buzz of his intercom blared in the room like the blast of a horn, seconds before his assistant's voice intruded. "Mr. Holloway, I'm sorry to interrupt. But you asked me to remind you about your two-o'clock meeting with the marketing team."

Ezekiel stared down at Reagan, his chest heaving, his breath like a chain saw. Equal parts shock and grinding lust tore at him, and *fuck*, where had this need come from? How had it burned out of control so fast?

Anything that uncontrollable, that hot, that addictive wasn't good. Not for him. Not when he needed to maintain that careful emotional distance. Not when she would possibly want more from him then he was able to give.

Yet…she'd come to him; she needed him. Maybe he couldn't help her obtain her inheritance, but he could unconditionally support her, be that person she could finally lean on. *Still rescuing her*, a voice that sounded suspiciously like his brother whispered through his head. Possibly. Probably. But, she'd assured him she didn't desire more than he was capable of offering, that she didn't love him. Obviously, she craved him as much as he did her—that combustible kiss confirmed that. And, as she'd just stormed in here and told him, she made her own decisions, knew her own mind.

If she did, then they could go through with this marriage, maybe, once Douglas calmed down, still have a chance to obtain her inheritance and have scorching-hot sex, too. He could have her and when the time came, walk away.

Because there were no ifs about that. He *would* walk away. As she would.

Slowly releasing her, he returned to his desk. Planting a hand on the desk, he looked at Reagan again. She hadn't moved, but gazed at him, mouth wet and puffy from his kisses.

Ezekiel pressed a button on his phone.

"Laura," he said to his executive assistant, "please cancel the meeting as well as clear and reschedule my calendar for the next week. I'm going to be out of the office. If anyone asks, I'm getting married."

Eleven

Good God, they'd done it.

As of two hours ago, she was Mrs. Reagan Holloway, Ezekiel Holloway's wife. She stared out the floor-to-ceiling window of the luxury suite into the bright, dazzling lights of the Las Vegas strip. Ezekiel hadn't spared any expense for the place they would spend their honeymoon.

Honeymoon. She wrestled with the emotions twisting and tumbling inside her. Jesus. This was unreal. As unreal as the whirlwind trip to Las Vegas after leaving his office twenty-four hours ago. As unreal as the unexpectedly lovely and private ceremony under a candlelit and crystal-encrusted gazebo in the back of a chapel made of glass. As unreal as this elegant and richly appointed penthouse with its Italian marble foyer, sunken living room and lavish master bedroom.

Was it how she'd imagined her wedding and honeymoon to be?

No.

It was better because it was all *her* choice.

Somehow, it didn't seem possible that just yesterday she'd rushed into Ezekiel's office and demanded he marry her. She winced, her fingers tightening around the stem of her wineglass. Thinking back on her uncharacteristically rash act, she still couldn't believe she'd done it.

Or that she'd kissed him.

Her belly executed a perfect swan dive as she lifted trembling fingers to her lips. A day later, and the imprint of his mouth was still on hers. He'd branded her. Years from now, she would no doubt still feel the pressure, the slight sting, the hungry possession of that kiss. What a sad commentary on her love life that it'd been better than the best sex she'd ever had. Ezekiel Holloway could own a woman's soul with his mouth. No wonder he'd never lacked for company. No wonder women vied for a chance to spend just hours in his bed. Or out of it, for that matter.

She needed to stop thinking about him and other women.

Or that before this evening ended, she and Ezekiel would be swept up in the throes of passion.

Whispers of nerves and curls of heat tangled together inside her belly, and she exhaled, trying to calm both. If that kiss was any indication, Ezekiel was well versed in sex. She, on the other hand, not so much. There had only been a couple of men she'd been with in the last ten years. And while the experiences had been nice— God, how anemic *nice* sounded—the encounters hadn't

melted her bones or numbed her brain as just a mating
of mouths with Ezekiel had. What would actual sex be
like between them? Would he find her lacking? What
if she—

"Stop it."

She whipped around at the softly uttered command,
a bit of the wine in her glass sloshing over the rim to
dot the back of her hand. Silently cursing herself for her
jumpiness, she lifted her hand to her mouth and sucked
the alcohol from her skin.

Her heart thumped against her rib cage as Ezekiel's
gaze dipped to her lips and hand. That green, hooded
gaze damn near smoldered, and it seized the breath
from her lungs.

Clearing her throat, she snatched her attention from
him and returned it to the almost overwhelming sight
of Vegas. Not that the view could abolish him from her
mind's eye.

He'd ditched the black suit jacket he'd worn to their
wedding, and the white shirt stretched over his wide
shoulders, emphasizing their breadth. The sky blue tie
had also been removed and the first few buttons undone, granting her a glimpse of the smooth brown skin
at his throat and over his collarbone. The shirt clung to
his hard, deep chest and flat, tapered waist. The black
slacks embraced his muscled, long legs and couldn't
hide their strength.

She would know that strength tonight. Intimately.

Her lashes lowered, and she blindly lifted the glass
to her lips again as her fingertips rose to her own collarbone and found the small scar there, rubbing over the
raised flesh.

"Stop what?" she belatedly replied, her voice no louder than a whisper.

He didn't immediately answer, but a stir of the air telegraphed his movement. A moment later, another touch from a larger, rougher finger replaced hers. She opened her eyes to meet his, even as he lightly caressed the mark marring her skin. She gasped, unable to hold it in.

Heat blasted from that one spot, spiraling through her like a blowtorch to her insides. It battled with the ice that tried to encase her. The ice of memories. Of pain beyond imagining.

His gaze lifted from just below her neck to meet her eyes, the intensity there so piercing, she wondered if patients going under the knife encountered the same trepidation. The same sense of overwhelming exposure and vulnerability.

"I've noticed you touch this place here..." He stroked the scar, and she couldn't prevent the small shiver from working its way through her frame. Fire and ice. Arousal and shame. They intertwined like lovers inside her stomach, mating in a dirty dance. "You did it that night on the balcony and at the cemetery. At your parents' home. And again in my office the day you came to see me. It's your tell, Ray. Whenever you're uncomfortable. Or nervous. Possibly even scared."

He swept one more caress over her skin before dropping his arm. But he didn't move back out of her personal space, didn't grant her breathing room. Every inhale carried his earthy but fresh scent—like a cool, brisk wind through a lush forest. She wanted to wrap herself in it. But his too perceptive observation froze her to the spot.

"So whatever you're thinking that has you feeling any of those emotions, stop it. Or tell me so I can take the fear away."

Her attempt at diversion hadn't worked last time, so she stuck to a believable half-truth. At least he hadn't asked her how she got the scar. That, she could never admit to him. Because it would involve telling him her most carefully guarded secret.

"Why?" she murmured.

"Why what?" he asked. "Why do I want to take away your fear?"

She nodded.

"Because I've seen it one too many times in your eyes in the last few weeks, and I don't like it," he said.

She stiffened, taken aback by his words. But he cocked his head to the side, his gaze narrowing on her.

"Are you offended because I said it or because I noticed?" He hummed in his throat, lifting a hand to her again. This time he traced the arc of her eyebrow, then stroked a teasing path down the bridge of her nose before sweeping a caress underneath her eye. "These gorgeous brown eyes? They tell everything you're feeling. Whether you're amused, irritated, frustrated, thoughtful or angry. In a world where people deceive and hide, you're a refreshing gift of an anomaly. Except..." He exhaled roughly, still brushing the tender skin above her cheekbone. "You have secrets, Reagan. Your eyes even betray that. I don't need to know what they are to know they hurt you, make you guard this beautiful heart."

He pressed two fingertips to her chest, directly over the pounding organ. The organ he called beautiful but one that had caused her so much pain and disillusionment.

The organ that even now beat harder for him.

Taking several moments, she studied the dark, slashing eyebrows, the vibrant, light green eyes that seemed to miss nothing, the sensual fullness of his mouth, the silky facial hair that framed his lips and covered his rock-hard jaw. Beautiful. Such a beautiful man.

And hers. At least for the next year.

Hers to touch. To take into her body. To lie next to.

But not to love. His heart belonged to a dead woman, and he had no intention of trying to reclaim it. He'd warned her of that early in their bargain. And this heat between them—this heat that threatened to incinerate rational thought and sense—it warned her that if she wasn't careful, she could once again be that reckless sixteen-year-old willing to throw caution to the wind for love.

She'd vowed never to be that girl again.

Once more she skimmed a finger over the scar at her collarbone. The one she'd earned just before she miscarried and lost her baby.

She courted danger now, with this arrangement with Ezekiel. But if she held tightly to the reminder that pain and love were two sides of the same coin, she wouldn't cross that line into heartbreak. Because she refused to give him her heart.

But her body? Oh, that he could have.

Meeting his unwavering gaze, she slowly set the glass of wine on the glass table behind her. She moved forward, circling around him and heading out of the room toward the luxurious master suite. A huge king-size bed dominated the middle of the room while a wall of windows granted a sprawling view of Vegas and the desert beyond. The small sitting area with two ornate chairs and a small glass table occupied one corner, and a dainty vanity filled the other. A closed door hid the cavernous and opulent bathroom with its double sinks, Jacuzzi tub and glass shower big enough to accommodate an entire sorority.

Yet, as she spun around to face the door, nothing in the bedroom captured her attention like the man in the entrance. With one shoulder propped against the frame and his hands in his suit pants pockets, he silently watched her. Waited.

They hadn't discussed consummating their marriage; she'd avoided the conversation, unsure if it would be wise to go there with him. No, it wasn't wise. But God, she wanted it.

Even though she trembled with nerves and foolish excitement, she stared at him as she slowly dragged down the side zipper on her simple but elegant sleeveless gown. The white satin loosened, and she slid the skinny strap down one arm, then removed the other. Heart thudding almost painfully in her chest and her breath so loud it echoed in her head, she pushed the material down until it bunched at her hips. A small shimmy, and the dress flowed down her legs to pool around her feet.

The urge to dive for the bed and hide beneath the covers rose strong and hard inside her, but she forced herself to stay still, clad only in a nude strapless bra, matching thong and sheer, lace-topped thigh-high stockings. Then, notching her chin up, she silently ordered her arms to remain by her side, her fingers to remain unclenched.

She couldn't do anything about the shiver that worked its way through her body though. Or the throbbing of her pulse at her neck. Or the gooseflesh that popped up along her arms.

Or the moisture that even now gathered in her sex, no doubt drenching her barely-there panties. All he would have to do was lower that penetrating gaze down her torso and center it between her thighs to see the evidence of his affect on her.

That knowledge both thrilled and unnerved her.

She lifted her gaze from the solid width of his chest, where she'd focused all of her attention while she'd performed her impromptu striptease. And, *oh God*, what she spied there.

Raw, animalistic lust. Those green eyes burned bright with it. An answering coil tightened low in her belly, and she pressed a palm to the ache. His gaze dropped, and when it flicked back up to hers, she couldn't contain the whimper that escaped her. So much heat. So much hunger.

Had anyone ever looked at her as if she were their sustenance, sanity and survival?

No. No one had. Not the few lovers she'd had.

Not even Gavin.

What did it say about her that Ezekiel owned her with that look? That if she'd harbored even the tiniest of doubts about giving herself to him, that needy, ravenous, *necessary* stare undid every snarled tangle of doubt?

Slowly, he straightened, removing his hands from his pockets, and stalked forward, eliminating the distance between them. He didn't stop until not even a breath could've slid between them.

The wall of his solid chest brushed her nipples, sending arcs of sizzling pleasure from the tips to the clenching, empty flesh between her damp thighs. His muscular thighs pressed to hers, and against her belly… She shuddered, desire striking her middle like a lightning bolt. His thick, hard cock burrowed against her belly, and before she could think better of tempting the beast, she ground herself against his mouthwatering length. More than anything, she wanted him to possess every part of her.

"Playing with fire, Ray?" One of his big hands gripped her hip. But not to control her. To jerk her closer. To roll those lean hips and give her more of what she'd just taken.

Her teeth sank into her bottom lip, her lashes fluttering. But when his fingers dived into her hair, clenching the strands and tugging so pinpricks scattered across her scalp, she opened her eyes, meeting his. He didn't handle her with kid gloves, didn't treat her like this demure, sheltered socialite or a fragile girl. And God, *she loved it*. Wanted more.

"I'm not playing," she breathed, stroking her hands up his strong back and digging her nails into the dense muscle there. "No games between us."

"No games," he repeated in that same grit-and-granite voice. "How novel an idea." He lowered his head and nipped at her bottom lip. Then soothed the minute sting with a sweep of his tongue.

She groaned, leaning her head back into his grasp.

"You've showed me this pretty little body, almost making me come with just the sight of you. But I want the words, sweetheart. Tell me you want this—*me*—in your bed. In your body. Tell me…" He bent his head, pressing his forehead to hers. His breath pulsed against her lips, and she could almost taste the dark delight of his kiss. "Tell me you won't regret this in the morning."

Rising on her toes, she grazed her mouth over his. Returned for a harder, wetter taste. His lips parted over hers, and their tongues tangled, curled, took. When she pulled free, their heated pants punctuated the air, resounded in her ears.

"I want you. In my bed. Beside me. Over me. Inside me. This is my decision, Zeke. Eyes wide open. I'll have no regrets about giving myself to you." *My body, but not my heart.* She silently added that vow as a promise to herself and to him. He wanted no strings attached with their union, so when they divorced in a year, no emotional entanglements existed.

Well, she wanted the same. She *needed* the same.

His groan rolled out of him, and his fingers fisted in her hair again, tugging her head back. He slid his mouth over her jaw, down her neck and gently bit the tendon that ran along its length. She clawed at his back, arching into him. Craving more of that primal touch. As if reading her mind, he raked his teeth along her shoulder, retracing the path with the smooth glide of his lips.

Desperation invaded her, and she slid her hands around his torso, attacking his shirt buttons. She'd released the top four when his mouth passed over the scar on her collarbone.

Stiffening, she curled her fingers around the sides of his shirt, the air snagged in her throat. Every instinct in her screamed to jerk away from both his caress and the memories. But when the tip of his tongue traced the raised flesh, she closed her eyes and a half cry, half sigh escaped her throat. He didn't pause in his ministrations, but his hold on her tightened, as if lending her his strength.

The urge to recoil evaporated, replaced by the need to lean into him, press her cheek to his chest. Let him all the way in, past her heavily guarded secrets and into her heart. She ruthlessly squelched that longing under the bootheel of reality, but she did withdraw just a bit and dip her head to seek his mouth. Lose herself in the wildness of him.

His palms cradled her face, taking while she gave and gave. A new urgency roiled within her, and she hurriedly finished unbuttoning his shirt and removing the offensive material from his shoulders and arms. Offensive because it barred her from touching all that glorious, taut skin.

Once more she tore her mouth away from his, this time so she could watch her hands smooth over his broad shoulders and wide chest with something close to wonder. So much strength, so much power. And vulnerability, she mused, scraping her nails over his small, dark brown nipples. He shivered, his clasp on her face shifting to her hips.

"Again," he ordered, grinding his erection into her belly. "And use your teeth this time."

The echo of dominance in that order had flames licking at her. She could do nothing else but obey. Not because he'd demanded it…but because she wanted it.

Lowering her head, she opened her mouth wide over the small, beaded tip, swirled a warm, wet caress around it, then raked her teeth on him. Gently biting and teasing. His rumbled curse pierced the air as a big hand cupped the back of her head and pressed her closer. Emboldened, she sucked and nipped, torturing both of them. She switched to the other tip, delivering the same caresses. By the time she drew on him one last time, fine tremors quaked through his big frame.

"Payback, sweetheart." He strode forward, forcing her to backpedal.

When the backs of her knees hit the edge of the mattress, she sank to the bed, and he immediately dropped to his knees in front of her, wedging himself between her legs.

Embarrassment flashed through her for a quick instant. In this vulnerable position, he had a clear shot of what he did to her. Her thong would hide nothing from him, and even now the cool air in the room kissed the dampness on her sex and high inside her thighs.

But all thoughts of modesty shattered into dust as he scattered hard, burning kisses to her stomach, the tops of her sensitive breasts and the shadowed valley between. He cupped her flesh with both hands, squeezing and molding, and pleasure howled through her. Tilting her head back, Reagan closed her eyes, savoring his sure touch. She curled her fingers into the covers beneath her hips, seeking purchase in this lust-whipped storm.

Peeling away the cups of her bra, he wasted no time tasting her just as she'd done him. His diabolical tongue curled around her nipple, stroking, sucking. Was it possible to be driven insane with pleasure? If so, the trip was more than halfway over for her.

Unable to *not* touch him any longer, she gripped his head in her hands, pressing him to her, staring down at him as he tormented her with that beautiful, wicked mouth. It was erotic—almost too sexual to behold. But she couldn't drag her gaze away.

As he shifted to her neglected breast, he whisked the

pad of his thumb over the aching, wet nipple, teasing it. His attention shifted from her quivering flesh up to her face, and their gazes locked. He didn't release her from the visual entrapment as he pursed his lips and pulled her into his mouth. Kept her enthralled as he lapped at her before drawing so hard the tug reverberated in her sex.

Too much. Too much.

She closed her eyes, but that was a mistake, because the lack of sight only enhanced the sizzling sensations crackling along her nerve endings.

With one last suck on her tip, he abandoned her breasts and trailed a blazing path down her stomach, briefly pausing to dip into her navel with a heated stroke, then continuing down, down, *oh God*, down.

His breath bathed her soaked flesh, and she tumbled back on the mattress, pressing the heels of her hands to her eyes. Instinct had her squeezing her thighs, but his palms prevented the motion. He spread her wider, and though she didn't look down, she swore she could *feel* his gaze on her. The heat of it. The intensity of it.

Pushing herself up, she balanced her weight on her elbows. Stared down her body as he hooked his fingers in the thin band of her panties and drew the scrap of material down her legs. Leaving her bare, exposed and completely vulnerable. But the fierce, undiluted hunger darkening his face banished those emotions. How could she feel vulnerable when he focused on her as if she were his sole purpose of existing in this moment? No, no. She didn't feel weak, she felt…empowered.

He wanted her just as much as she wanted him.

His thumb stroked between her folds, and she glimpsed how it glistened with the proof of her desire.

Lifting his gaze to hers, Ezekiel brought his thumb to his mouth and licked it clean. If possible, his magnificent features tightened further, and an almost animalistic sound rumbled from him. Then he put his mouth on her.

A keening wail tore free from her throat as he dived into her sex. His tongue licked the same path his thumb had taken. Again and again, lapping at her. Devouring her. Destroying her. His hum of pleasure vibrated against her sensitive, swollen flesh, and she writhed beneath him. He left no part of her undiscovered, staking his claim on her as thoroughly as if he'd branded her. His lips closed around the bundle of nerves at the top of her sex, and he carefully drew on her, his tongue swirling, rubbing and teasing.

Desperate and coming undone, she settled her heels on the edge of the bed, widening her thighs and grinding into his relentless mouth. Electrical currents danced up and down her spine, and for a moment, she feared the power of this looming orgasm. Even as the pleasure swelled, she mentally scrambled back from it. Both wanting it to break and fearing the breaking.

But Ezekiel didn't grant her any quarter. He slid a finger and then another through her folds, then slowly pushed them inside her. Her sex immediately clamped down on them, and she cried out, arching hard, her hips twisting, bearing down. Pleading for more of that invasion. That fulfillment. Again, her mind whispered *too much*, but this time she didn't run from it but embraced it. She worked her hips, sexing his fingers even as she pushed into his mouth.

More. More. More.

"Take it then, sweetheart," Ezekiel encouraged her,

and she realized she'd chanted the demand aloud. "Give it to me."

His urging and the stroking of his fingertips over a place high and deep inside her catapulted her into orgasm. She exploded, her cries bouncing off the walls, and he didn't stop, not until she weakly pushed at his head, her flesh too sensitive.

Lethargy rolled over her in a wave, and she sprawled on the mattress, unable to move. She could only stare as Ezekiel surged to his feet and quickly stripped himself of his remaining clothes.

Her breath stuttered as he bared that big, hard, gorgeous body. She'd already caressed and kissed his wide chest. But his lean hips, that V above them designed to drive women wild with lust, his powerful, muscular thighs, and God, his dick. Long, thick and wide, the swollen tip reached to just under his navel. Maybe she should feel some kind of trepidation at taking him inside her. But no, with the renewed rush of desire flooding her veins, she craved having him fill her. She ached for it. Maybe then this emptiness would dissipate.

Ezekiel paused to grab his wallet from his pants before tossing them aside. From the depths of the black leather billfold, he withdrew a couple of small square foils and tossed one on the bed before ripping open the other.

She waited for him, equal parts eagerness and nerves. There was no turning back—not that she wanted to. She didn't fool herself into believing there wouldn't be consequences for this decision. For both of them.

Yet, as he sheathed himself and climbed on the bed, crawling over her body, she didn't care about the costs. Not when his gaze burned into hers. Not when he settled between her thighs. Not when he cradled her face between his large palms.

Not when his cock nudged her entrance and slowly penetrated her.

She gasped at the welcome, coveted intrusion. Whimpered at the low-level fire of the stretching. Clutched his shoulders at the unmistakable sense of being claimed.

"Zeke," she whispered, burrowing her face into the nook between his throat and shoulder. "Please."

She shifted restlessly beneath him, unsure how to alleviate the pressure that contained both pleasure and the barest bite of pain. It'd been so long for her, that as he pushed, steadily burying himself inside her, she couldn't remain still. Had to find the position, the place that would relieve the ache…or agitate it more.

"Shh," he soothed, tilting her head up and brushing his mouth across hers. "Relax for me, Ray." Another stroke of his lips even as he continued to gain more access to her body, drive farther inside her. "Relax and take me. That's it," he praised, momentarily closing his eyes as she lifted her legs around his waist, locking her ankles at the small of his back. Allowing him to surge deeper. "Fuck, that's good, sweetheart. So good," he ground out.

He held himself still above her, only his mouth moving over hers, his tongue mimicking his possession of her body. She returned every kiss, losing herself in him. Gradually, the hint of pain subsided, and only pleasure remained. Pure, mind-bending pleasure.

On a gasp, she arched her neck, pressing her head back into the mattress. Savoring him buried so deep inside her. Impatience rippled through her, and she rocked her hips, demanding he move. Demanding he take her.

Levering off her chest, he stared down at her, green eyes bright, expression dark.

"Ready?" he growled.

"Yes," she murmured, curling her hands around his strong upper arms. "Please."

With his attention pinned on her face, he withdrew his length, the weightiness of it dragging over newly awakened nerves. She groaned, twisting beneath him. Needing more. Hating how empty she felt when she'd just been so full. But a jerk of his hips granted her wish. He plunged back inside her with a force that stole the air from her lungs, the thoughts from her head.

Over and over, he took her, thrusting, driving, riding. On the end of each stroke, he ground his hips against her so he massaged that swollen bundle of nerves cresting the top of her sex. She'd become a sexual creature void of rational thought, only craving the ecstasy each plunge inside her promised. She raced after it, writhing and bucking beneath him, demanding he give her everything, hold nothing back from her.

And he didn't.

Crushing his mouth to hers, he reached between their straining, sweat-slicked bodies and circled her clitoris, once, twice, and before he could finish the third stroke, she shattered.

She came with a scream, throwing her head back, body quaking with wave after wave of release. For a second, she fought the power of it. But as he continued to thrust into her, riding out the orgasm so she received every measure of it, she submitted to the pleasure, to the loss of control.

And as she dived into the black abyss, she didn't hesitate or worry.

Because she knew, at least for the moment, she wasn't alone.

Twelve

As Ezekiel steered his Jaguar up the quiet Pine Valley street, he glanced at his wife. *His wife.* He rubbed a hand over his beard before returning it to the steering wheel. Part of him still couldn't believe he could call Reagan Sinclair—no, Reagan Holloway—by that title. Not just bride. That ship had sailed when she led him to their master bedroom and stripped for him in a private show that had him nearly begging to put his hands on that pretty body. Stroke all that smooth, beautiful skin. Taste her mouth and the sweet flesh between her thighs.

He probably shouldn't be thinking about sex with his wife while driving down the road to his in-laws' house to drop some unwelcome news.

Especially when just the thought of Reagan naked beneath him, eyes glazed over with pleasure, her sensual demands for *more* pouring from her kiss-swollen lips, had him shifting uncomfortably in his seat.

Two days. He should've been back to Royal and Wingate Enterprises two days ago. They were supposed to fly to Vegas, tie the knot, then fly back. But after that first night with Reagan, drowning in an unprecedented lust that had seared him from the inside out, he'd extended their "honeymoon." They'd spent it in the suite. Talking. Laughing. Eating. Fucking.

And sleeping.

For the first time since Melissa, he'd slept beside a woman instead of leaving her bed or guiding her from his. And the guilt he'd expected to flay him alive had been absent. Which had only stirred the flood of conscience and shame that had been missing.

But not enough to drag him from his wife's bed or make him uncurl himself from around her warm, naked body to sleep on the couch. Because then she wouldn't be within easy reach when he woke up throbbing and hard for her.

It appeared he couldn't get enough of his new wife. In and out of bed. Although to be fair, they hadn't gone very far from the bed.

He smothered a sigh. Okay, so they'd crossed the platonic bridge and burned it in a blaze of glory behind them. But he hadn't lost complete control over this situation. They could carry on with their plan of living separate lives without emotional entanglements. Sex did blur the line a little, but it didn't obliterate it.

He and Reagan had set those boundaries for very good reasons.

And neither of them could afford to forget those reasons.

A kernel of unease wiggled into his chest. She'd already made him forget his priorities—saving Wingate Enterprises. He couldn't allow this kind of slip to become a habit.

Beside him, Reagan fidgeted. And not for the first or fifth time. Glancing down, he noticed her clenched fists on her lap. Before he could question the wisdom of it, he covered her hands with one of his and squeezed.

"It's going to be okay," he murmured.

She shook her head, a faint, wry smile tipping the corner of her mouth. "I ran off to Vegas with a man my parents disapprove of. I don't know which will send my mother into a coronary faster—the elopement or Vegas. And my father..." She shook her head, releasing a humorless chuckle. "I don't even want to imagine his reaction right now. I started all of this to take my inheritance and keep my family. But it might turn out that I lose both."

"You're borrowing trouble, Ray," Ezekiel said softly. "Your father might be stern and overbearing, but he loves you. He'll stand by you."

She huffed out a breath. "You don't know Douglas Sinclair. Not like I do. If there's one thing experience has taught me it's that he doesn't handle disappointment well. And he never, *ever* forgets."

He jerked his gaze from the road to throw her a sharp look. Something in her voice—bitterness, sorrow, pain... It wasn't the first time he'd detected that particular note, just as he'd noted her habitual stroking of that scar just below her neck.

Secrets. And if he was staring into her eyes, he would see the shadows of them there.

Moments later, her parents' home loomed into view

and he steered the car up the driveway, pulling to a stop in front of the mansion.

"Reagan." He waited until she switched her gaze from the side window to him. "Whatever you face in there, I will be right beside you. I won't leave you."

Her lips twisted into a smile that in no way reached her eyes. They remained dark. Sad. The urge to demand she pour out her pain onto him, to insist she let him in swelled within him, shoving against his chest and throat. But before he could speak, she nodded and reached for the door handle.

"We should go in," she murmured, pushing the door open and stepping out.

Silent, he met her in front of the car and took hold of her hand. The warning to not muddy the boundaries rebounded against his skull as he raised her hand to his lips and brushed a kiss across the back of it. She glanced at him, and a glint of desire flickered in her eyes. Good. Anything to chase away the shadows.

Just as they cleared the top step, the front door opened, and Douglas Sinclair stood in the entrance. He stared at them, his scrutiny briefly dropping to their clasped hands before shifting back to his daughter.

He didn't greet them but moved backward and held the door open wider. Yet, nothing about his grim expression was welcoming. More likely he didn't want the neighbors to have a free show.

Settling a hand on Reagan's lower back, Ezekiel walked inside, lending her his strength. He valued family loyalty and acceptance. Understood the drive to give one and crave the other. Yet he hated how even while Reagan strode ahead, shoulders soldier-straight, head tilted at a proud angle, she did so with a fine tremor that echoed through her and into his palm.

"Reagan." Henrietta rose from the couch as soon as they entered the small salon. She crossed the room and cupped her daughter's shoulders, pressing a kiss to her cheek. "Where have you been? We've been calling you for days now. Honey, we were all so worried."

"I'm sorry, Mom," Reagan said, covering one of her mother's hands and patting it. "I had my phone turned off. I didn't mean to scare you."

Henrietta studied her daughter for a long moment before shifting her scrutiny to Ezekiel. "Ezekiel," she greeted with a nod. "It's good to see you again."

"You, too, Henrietta," he replied, slipping his hand up Reagan's spine to cup the nape of her neck.

"Mom, Dad, I have news," Reagan announced. "Zeke and I—" She broke off, and he squeezed the back of her neck, silently reassuring her. "Zeke and I are married. We eloped to Las Vegas. I'm sorry that you're finding out after the fact, but we—"

"I asked her to come away with me, and she did," he interjected, but she shook her head, giving him a small but sad smile.

"No, he didn't. I asked him, and I know you're probably disappointed in my decision to elope, but it was my decision." She squared her shoulders. "*He* is my decision."

Surprise and no small amount of hurt flashed across her mother's face, but the older woman quickly composed her features. She shifted backward until she stood next to Douglas, who hadn't spoken. But his stern, forbidding frown might as well as have been a lecture.

Every protective instinct buried inside Ezekiel

clawed its way to the surface, and he faced the other man, moving closer to Reagan. Letting it be known that she was his. And dammit, whether that claim had an expiration date or not, he would protect what was his.

"You deliberately went against my wishes, and now you show up here for, what?" Douglas demanded, his voice quiet thunder. "For our blessing? Our forgiveness? Acceptance? Well, you have none of them."

"No, not your blessing," Ezekiel said evenly, but he didn't bother hiding the steel or the warning in it. "And she nor I require forgiveness for a choice we made together as two consenting adults. Would your acceptance of our marriage be important to your daughter? Yes. But it's not necessary."

"It is if she—or you—want access to her inheritance," Douglas snapped. "Which isn't going to happen. Her grandmother gave me final say over who I deem suitable, and you are not it. Reagan knew that and yet she still defied my wishes, regardless that it would bring hurt and shame onto her family."

"Douglas," Henrietta whispered, laying a hand on her husband's arm.

"No, Henrietta, this needs to be said," he said. "I—"

"No, it doesn't," Reagan quietly interrupted. "It doesn't need to be said, Dad, because I already know. You've made it very clear over the years—ten to be exact—that I have only brought disappointment, embarrassment and pain to this family. God knows I've tried to make up for it by being the respectable, obedient daughter, by following every rule you've laid down, by placing your needs and opinions above my own. But nothing I've done or will do will ever make up for me being less than worthy of the Sinclair name. For being less than perfect."

"Honey," Henrietta breathed, reaching a hand toward her daughter. "That's just not true."

That sense of foreboding spread inside Ezekiel, triggering the need to gather Reagan into his arms and shield her from the very people who were supposed to love her unconditionally. Because this was about more than an elopement or an inheritance. This—whatever it was that vibrated with pain and ugliness between these three—was older, burrowed deeper. And it still bled like a fresh wound.

"It's true, Mom," Reagan continued in that almost eerily calm voice. "We've just been so careful not to voice it aloud."

Ezekiel looked at Douglas, silently roaring at the man to say something, to comfort his obviously hurting daughter. To climb down off that high horse and tell her she was loved and accepted. Valued.

"If you think this 'woe is me' speech is going to change my mind about the inheritance, you're wrong." The same deep freeze in Douglas's voice hardened his face. "I hope your new *husband...*" he sneered the word "...with his own financial and legal troubles can provide for you. Although, that future is looking doubtful."

Fury blazed through Ezekiel, momentarily transforming his world into a crimson veil.

"Watch it, Douglas," he warned. "No one smears my family name. And since your daughter now wears it, she's included. I care for mine... I protect them above all else. And before you throw that recklessly aimed stone, you might want to ask yourself if you can claim the same."

"Don't you dare question me about how I protect my family," Douglas snapped. "All I have ever done, every decision, is for them. You, who has had everything handed to you merely because of your last name, know nothing about sacrifice. About the hard work it takes to ensure your family not only survives but thrives. About rising above what people see in order to be more than they ever believed you are possible of. You don't know any of that, Ezekiel *Holloway.* So don't you ever question my love for them. Because it's that love that convinces me that my daughter marrying you is the worst decision she could've ever made."

Anger seethed beneath Ezekiel's skin, a fiercely burning flame that licked and singed, leaving behind scorch marks across his heart and soul.

"I may be a Holloway, but I'm still a black man in Royal, Texas. You don't corner the market on that. When the world looks at me, they don't see my white father. They see a black man who should be grateful about being born into a powerful, white family. When they find out where I work and my position, they assume I'm only there because I'm Ava Holloway Wingate's nephew, not because I earned it by busting my ass working my way up in the company while attending college and receiving my bachelor's and master's." He huffed out a breath. "So don't talk to me about hard work or sacrifice, because I've had to surrender my voice and my choice at times so others can feel comfortable about sitting down at a table with me. I've had to work ten times harder just to be in the same place and receive the respect that others are given just because of the color of their skin."

He forced his fingers to straighten from the fist

they'd curled into down by his thigh. "And I never questioned your love for your family. I just have reservations about the way you show it."

"Zeke," Reagan whispered, leaning into him. Offering support or comfort, he didn't know. Maybe both.

"Please, if we can all just calm down for a moment," Henrietta pleaded, glancing from her husband and back to Ezekiel and Reagan. "Before we all say something we can't take back."

"Mom, I'm afraid it's too late for that," Reagan said, a weariness that Ezekiel detested weighing down every word. "And I'm sorry for hurting you. Again." Inhaling a deep breath, she dipped her chin in her father's direction. "You, too, Dad."

She turned and walked out of the room, and Ezekiel followed, not giving her parents a backward glance. His loyalty belonged to the woman they'd just selfishly, foolishly rejected.

Fuck it. He would be her family now.

She had him. And no matter that their union was temporary, he would give her a family to belong to.

Thirteen

Funny how a person could have pain pouring from every cell of their body and still walk, breathe, *live*. Since arriving at her parents' house, she'd become the embodiment of agony, grief and rage. Yet, she managed to grab an overnight bag, descend the front steps, climb into Ezekiel's car, buckle up and not break down as he drove away from a house that had been her home all her life.

Like a horror-movie reel, the scene in the informal parlor played out across her mind. Only to rewind when it finished and start again.

Reagan squeezed her eyes shut and balled her hands in her lap. But all that did was twist the volume up in her head. She'd known deep down that her father blamed her for her past mistakes, had never forgiven her for them. And his accusations as well as his stony silence confirmed it. But still, oh God, did that *hurt*. It hurt so badly she longed to curl up in a ball on the passenger's seat and just disappear.

Be strong.

Never show weakness or emotion.

Be above reproach and avoid the very appearance of impropriety.

Those had been rules, creeds she'd lived by as a Sinclair. And except for when she'd fallen so far from grace at sixteen, she'd striven to live up to that hefty responsibility. But now, after living with so many cracks and fissures because of the pressure placed on her, she just wanted to break. Break into so many pieces until Reagan Sinclair could never be formed again.

Then who would be left? Who would she be?

God, she didn't know. And how pathetic was that?

"Reagan." Ezekiel's voice penetrated the thick, dark morass of her thoughts, and she jerked her head up. He stood in the opening of her car door. A car she hadn't realized he'd stopped and pulled over, and a door she hadn't heard him open. "Come on out."

He extended his hand toward her, his green eyes, so full of concern, roaming over her face. Slowly, she slid her palm over his and allowed him to guide her from the vehicle. Only then did she notice he'd parked on the side of a quiet, deserted road.

She recognized it. Several country roads twisted through Royal, some leading to the ranches that dotted the town and others leading to rolling fields filled with wildflowers. This one lay several miles outside her parents' gated community. A bend in the road and a thick copse of trees shielded them from anyone who might travel past the end of it. As Ezekiel closed the door behind her, turned her so he rested against the Jaguar and pulled her into his arms, she was thankful for the semi-privacy.

"Go ahead, sweetheart," he murmured against her head as he wrapped his arms around her, one big hand tunneling through her hair and pressing her to his chest. "Let it go. No one can see you here. Let it go because I have you."

The emotional knot inside her chest tightened, as if her body rebelled against the loosening storm inside of her. But in the next moment, the dam splintered, and the torrent spilled out. A terrible, jagged sob wracked her frame, and she buried her face against Ezekiel's chest as the first flood of tears broke through.

Once she started, she couldn't stop. How long she wept for that sixteen-year-old girl who'd been abandoned by the boy she'd loved and her family, Reagan couldn't say. It seemed endless, and yet, seconds. Fists twisted in his shirt, she clung to him, because at this moment, he was her port in a storm that had been brewing for years.

Eventually, she calmed, her harsh cries quieting to silent tears that continued to track down her cheeks. And even they stopped. Ezekiel cupped one of her hands and pressed a handkerchief into it.

"Thank you," she rasped, the words sore against her raw throat.

He stroked her back as she cleaned up the ravages of her weeping jag.

"I'm here if you want to talk. Or if you don't want to talk. Your choice, Reagan," he murmured.

The self-preservation of her family's demand for secrecy—as well as her own guilt—battled the urge to unload. But God, she was tired. So tired. Yes, she struggled with trusting people, in trusting herself. Maybe, just maybe, she could try to take a little leap of faith and trust him…

"When I was sixteen, I was involved with a boy— well, he was nineteen years old. My parents didn't approve of him. And in hindsight, I understand why. But back then, I was just so hopelessly in love with him and would've done anything for him. And I did. I rebelled against Dad and Mom. I saw him behind their backs, sneaked out at night to see him. He consumed my world as a first love usually does. But…" she swallowed, closing her eyes "…I ended up pregnant."

Ezekiel stiffened against her, and she braced herself for his reaction. Shock. Disbelief. Pity. Any or all of them would be like a punch to her chest.

He shifted, settling more against his car and drawing her between his spread thighs. Pulling her deeper into his big, hard body. Gentle but implacable fingers gripped her chin and tilted her head back.

"Open your eyes, sweetheart. Look at me."

She forced herself to comply, and her breath snagged in her lungs. Compassion. Tenderness. Sorrow. But no pity. No disappointment.

"You have nothing to be ashamed of, so don't look down while you give me your truth."

She stared at him. *Nothing to be ashamed of.* No one—not her parents, not her brother or sister—had ever said those words to her. But this man did. Against his wishes, she briefly closed her eyes. That or allow him to glimpse the impact of his assurance. He'd said her eyes reflected her feelings, and she didn't even want to identify the emotion that had her mentally backpedaling. Had fear rattling her ribs and clenching her stomach.

Shoving everything into a lockbox deep inside her, she drew in a breath and lifted her lashes, meeting that piercing green gaze.

"As you can expect, my parents didn't react well to the news. And yes, I was terrified. Yet I also believed my boyfriend when he said he would never leave me. What I hadn't counted on was that dedication not measuring up against the check my father waved in front of his face. Dad paid him off, and he disappeared. And my parents... They sent me away. To a girls' home in Georgia."

"I remember," Ezekiel said. "It was just before the school year ended, and Harley was upset because you wouldn't be with her for the summer. She never mentioned—"

"She didn't know," Reagan interrupted, shaking her head. "No one except my family did. My parents didn't want anyone to find out. I was supposed to go to the home, have the baby and adopt him or her out. I didn't want to give my baby up, but they were adamant. They were embarrassed and ashamed." The words tasted like ash on her tongue. "Especially my father. Before, we'd been close. I was a self-admitted daddy's girl, and there was no man greater than my father in my eyes. But afterward... He couldn't even look at me," she whispered.

"And this?" He gently pushed her fingers aside— the fingers that had been absently rubbing the scar on her collarbone.

"When I was about fourteen weeks, I started cramping. I didn't tell anyone for the first couple of days. But the third morning, pain seized my lower back so hard I doubled over and almost fainted. I did fall, and on the way down I clipped myself on the dresser." She again stroked the mark that would forever remind her of the worst day of her life. "I lay there on the floor, curled up, bleeding from the wound when I felt a—a wetness between my legs. I was miscarrying."

"Oh, Ray," Ezekiel whispered, lowering his forehead to hers, and his breath whispered across her lips. "I'm sorry."

"Spontaneous miscarriage, they called it," she continued, needing to purge herself of the whole truth. To cleanse herself of the stain of secrecy. "They told me there was nothing I could've done to prevent it, but I still felt responsible. That it was my punishment for disobeying my parents, for not being the daughter they deserved, for having unprotected sex, for not being good enough for my boyfriend to stay around, to love me—"

"Sweetheart, no," he objected fiercely, his brows drawing down in a dark frown as his head jerked back. "None of that is true. It happens. My mother suffered two miscarriages. One before me and one after me. It happens to good people, to women who would've made wonderful, loving mothers. It was biological, not penal." Worry flashed in his eyes. "Were you hurt more than you're telling me?"

"Do you mean can I still have children? Yes." Relief swept away the concern from his expression, but she shook her head. "But do I want to? I—I don't know." It was a truth she'd never admitted aloud. "It may have happened ten years ago, but the pain, the fear, the grief, the terrible emptiness…" She pressed a palm to her stomach. "I'll never forget it. And I'm terrified of suffering that again. I don't want to. Losing another child…" She turned her head away from his penetrating stare. "I don't know if I can."

"Reagan. Sweetheart. Will you look at me?"

Several heartbeats passed, but she returned her gaze to him.

He circled a hand around her nape, a thumb stroking the side of her neck while the other hand continued to cup her face. "You don't have to explain or justify anything to me. I get it. After my parents and then Melissa died, the thought of loving another person only to lose them to illness, fate or death paralyzes me. They don't give out handbooks explaining that one day that person might be snatched unfairly from us. No one prepared me for that, just as no one prepared you for the fact that you might lose your baby before you had the chance to hold him or her. And because no one did, we only get to dictate how we deal."

He stroked the pad of his thumb over her cheekbone, his gaze softening.

"Do I think you would one day make a beautiful, caring and attentive mother who would love your child as fiercely as the most protective mama bear? Yes. Do I believe you deserve to know the feeling of cradling a child in your arms, smelling their scent, hearing him calling you Mom? Yes, sweetheart. You deserve all of that and more. But I'm the last person to tell you you're wrong for being afraid of it. And Reagan…?"

He paused, his scrutiny roaming her face, alighting on her mouth, nose and finally eyes. She *felt* his tender survey like caresses on her skin. "If no one else has ever told you, I'm sorry. I'm sorry for the loss of your baby. I'm sorry the boy—because he's not worthy of the title of man—you believed would stand by you abandoned you instead. I'm sorry that you felt deserted by your family. And I'm sorry no one told you that in spite of—no, *because* of—your life lessons, you are even more precious."

The need to reassure him that he, too, deserved more trembled on her tongue. Ezekiel deserved a woman who adored him beyond reason. Who would be his soft place to land as well as the rock he leaned on in times of trouble. The thought of him alone, with the heart he so zealously guarded as his only companion, saddened her more than she could vocalize without betraying emotion either of them would be comfortable with.

So instead, she rose on her toes and pressed her mouth to his. Tried to convey her gratitude for his compassion and kindness. Attempted to relay everything she was too confused to say aloud.

Immediately, his lips parted under hers. His hold on her cheek slid into her hair, and his fingernails scraped her scalp, arrowing shivers of heat directly to her breasts, belly and lower, between her thighs.

Sorrow and hurt morphed to heat, kindling the desire inside her that never extinguished. Not for him. For Ezekiel Holloway, she was a pilot light that never went out.

His groan vibrated against her chest, then rolled into her mouth. She greedily swallowed it, the emotional turmoil of the last hour spurring her on to drown in him and this overwhelming pleasure that bore his personal stamp of ownership.

"Ray." He moaned her name, but his hands dropped to her shoulders as if to push her away. "Sweetheart."

"No," she objected. Stroking her hands over his hips and up his back, she curled her fingers into his shirt.

Held on and pulled him tighter against her. "I want you. I want this. Don't deny me, Zeke," she said.

Demanded.

Pleaded.

His gaze narrowed on her, studying her. After the longest of moments, he shifted, spinning them around so she perched on the hood of the Jaguar and he stood between her spread thighs.

He flattened his palms on the metal beside her, leaning forward until she placed her hands next to his and arched her head back.

"I won't deny you anything," he growled.

Then his mouth crushed hers.

He hated the words as soon as he let them slip. Wanted to snatch them back. They revealed too much, when he should've been protecting his tender underbelly from exposure.

But with lust a ravenous beast clawing at his insides, he couldn't care right now. Not when her tongue dueled with his, sucking at him as if she couldn't get enough of him. Nipping at him as if she wanted to mark him. Licking him as if he were a flavor that both teased and never satisfied.

He should know.

Because as he sucked, nipped and licked her, all three were true for him.

This woman… *Goddamn*. She was ruining him with her sinful mouth, wicked tongue and hungry moans. Even now, he couldn't remember another's kiss, another's scent. Another's touch. And that traitorous thought should anger him, fill him with guilt. And maybe later it would. But now? Now, all he could do was dig his fingers through her hair, fist the thick strands and hold her steady for a tongue-fucking that had his dick throbbing for relief.

Nothing else mattered but her and getting inside her.

With fingers that were miraculously steady, he swept them over her jaw, down her throat, lingered on the scar that carried such traumatic memories for her and lower to the simple bow at her waist that held the top of her wrap dress together. He tugged on the knot, loosening it, and didn't hesitate to smooth his palms inside the slackened sides to push the material off her shoulders and down her arms to pool around her wrists.

Reagan started to lift her arms, but he stilled the movement. Instead, he gripped her wrists and pulled them behind her back. Trapped by her dress and his firm fingers, back arched, she was a gorgeous, vulnerable sacrifice for him. Only, as he lowered his head to drag his tongue down the middle of her chest to the shadowed, sweetly scented valley between her breasts, he was the one eager and willing to throw himself on the altar of his need for her.

God, he couldn't get enough of her taste. That honeysuckle scent seemed entrenched in her smooth, beautiful brown skin, and he was a treasure hunter, constantly returning for more.

Tracing the inner curve of her breast, he couldn't resist raking his teeth over it and satisfaction roared through him at the shiver that worked through her body. He'd earned a PhD in the shape and map of her body in the last few days, and yet, every time he discovered a new area that caused her to quake or whimper, he wanted to throw back his head and whoop in victory.

He'd never get tired of eliciting new reactions from her, of giving her new things to shatter over.

And that was a problem since he was letting her go in a year.

Smothering the thought that tried to intrude on the desire riding him, he refocused all of his attention on the flesh swelling above the midnight blue lace of her bra. And the hard tip beneath it. Bringing his free hand into play, he tugged down the cup, baring her breast to him. Then, pinching and teasing the silk-and-lace-covered nipple, he drew its twin into his mouth.

He couldn't contain his rumble of pleasure as he stroked, lapped and sucked on her. Part of him believed he was obsessed with her—the last four days pointed toward this. His preoccupation now further emphasized it. How he took his time circling the beaded nub, re-learning her although he'd just had her before they left their suite that morning to board the plane home.

The other part of him wanted to get down on his knees and beg her to push him away, ban him from her bed so he could wean himself off an addiction that could only destroy them both in the end.

"Zeke," Reagan gasped, twisting and arching up to him, thrusting her flesh into his mouth. Demanding her pleasure. "I need you," she said on the tail end of a whimper.

Fuck if he didn't love that sound from her. Every needy, insatiable sound that telegraphed her hunger for him.

As he'd said before, he couldn't deny her anything.

Shifting his head, he freed the other breast and re-introduced it to his mouth. Over and over he tongued the tip, swirling and teasing, pulling and worshipping.

Because she *deserved* to be worshipped.

And not just because of this body that could make a grown man find religion. But because she had a strength of spirit and character as well as a spine of steel underneath the genteel socialite demeanor. Because she'd taken her own tragedy and now planned to offer a safe haven to girls who faced the same difficulties.

Because she was just *good*.

Inexplicably, desperation surged through him, and he reached around her to unhook her bra and then rid her of both it and the top still trapping her wrists. He didn't question the need to feel her arms wrapped around him; he just surrendered to it.

He didn't even know how to begin to articulate the request—but simply grasped her hands and drew them forward, clasping them behind his neck. Then he buried his face in the crook between her throat and shoulder, inhaling her scent, opening his mouth over that sensitive spot, savoring the crush of her chest to his.

Yes, he'd been with more women than he could place names and faces to, but none had *held* him. He hadn't allowed it. And now, with Reagan, he craved it as much as he needed to be buried balls-deep inside her. And that need had him backing away from her mentally and physically, his ingrained self-protective instinct kicking him in the chest.

"Zeke?" she murmured, but he stopped the question with his mouth, and anything she would've asked translated into a groan.

As their mouths engaged in a hot, dirty battle, she gripped the front of his shirt and tackled his buttons. Within seconds, she tossed his shirt onto the hood behind him and raked her nails down his bare chest. Over his nipples. Down his abs. To the waistband of his pants.

The air in his lungs sawed in and out as she tugged at his leather belt, loosening it, then opened the closure tab. He didn't stop her—could barely drag in a damn full breath, much less move—when she lowered his zipper and dipped her hand inside his black boxer briefs.

He hissed as her fingers closed around his length, bowing his head so his cheek pressed to hers and he fisted the skirt of her dress. Pleasure spiked up his spine, locking his body. Gritting his teeth, he dipped his head lower, staring at the erotic sight of her slender, elegant fingers curled around his dick. The tips nearly-but-not-quite met around his width, and the brutish, swollen head peeked above her hand. As both of them watched, his seed pearled, and he damn near choked as she spread the drop over his flesh.

Ezekiel almost came on the spot when she lifted her thumb and slid it between her lips.

"What are you trying to do to me, Reagan?" he grunted, taking her mouth and licking deep. "You want this to end before I even get inside you?" He nipped her full bottom lip in punishment. "You want to see me lose it?"

The question sounded close to an accusation, and a small, utterly wicked smile teased her lips. "Yes. I want you to come *undone* for me."

And then she took him in her hand again, stroking him from tip to base. Squeezing. Up and down, her fist rode him, dragging him to the edge. Undoing him just as she'd claimed.

His stomach caved with each tight caress, each twist

of her fist. Bolt after hot bolt of lust attacked him, sizzling through his veins and gathered in his sac. So close. So fucking close.

But he didn't want to spill on her hand. When that happened, there was only one place he wanted to be.

Deep inside her.

Grabbing his wallet from his back pocket, he removed a condom and, in record time, sheathed himself, gritting his teeth against the pressure rapidly building inside him. With hands that should've been rough and hurried but were instead reverent and gentle, he swept higher and higher up her thighs until he reached her lace-covered sex.

For a moment, the lust almost overwhelmed him, drove him to grab, tug and claim. *Possess.* But his affection for her tempered the urge, and he eased her underwear from her with exquisite care. His concern for her had him slip his discarded shirt under her back to protect her skin from the warm metal of the car. His longing for her had him palming her thighs, holding her wide for his ravenous gaze and hard flesh as he pushed inside her. Watching her open for him, welcome him.

He glanced up her torso, over her trembling breasts to her face. And had to grab ahold of his frayed control with a desperate grip when he found her gaze trained on them joined between her legs, too.

"You see how you're taking me, sweetheart?" he whispered. Her eyes flicked to his and the heat there set a match to the already blazing conflagration in his body. "Perfect. You were made to do it. And I was created to fill you."

He didn't speak anymore...couldn't. Everything in him—every muscle, tendon, cell—focused on burying himself in the tightest, sweetest flesh. Tremors quivered through him, and he fought the need to thrust like a wild animal.

"Don't hold back from me, Zeke," she breathed, lying back on the hood and smoothing her palms down her body to cover his hands over her toned thighs. "Come. *Undone.*"

Her wish, her order snapped the cord tethering his control. He fell over her, pulling a taut nipple into his mouth as he thrust inside her over and over. Her legs and arms cradled him, her hips rising and bucking to meet each stroke. And her hoarse, primal cries for *more* spurred him on as he rode her.

Thank God.

He hoped if she'd asked him to stop, he would be able to. He prayed he would've managed it. But with her nails digging into his bare shoulders, the heels of her shoes pressed into his ass, he was so goddamn glad that fortitude wouldn't be tested. Not when sweat dotted his skin, lust strung him tighter than a drum, and pleasure barreled down on him like a train with greased tracks and no brakes.

"Let go, sweetheart," he rumbled, levering off her to reach between them and rub the swollen little nub at the top of her clenching sex.

She bowed hard, and seconds later, her core clamped down on him, nearly bruising him in her erotic embrace. She milked him, coaxing his release, and with several short, hard thrusts, he gave it to her.

Gave it to *them.*

A bone-deep lethargy swept through him, and right under it hummed a satisfaction that burrowed even deeper. Easing off Reagan, he took care of the condom, helped her dress and then righted himself. They didn't speak, but they did communicate. She clasped his hands in hers, brushing her lips over his chin and jaw. And he took her mouth, relaying how beautiful and desirable he found her.

Long moments later, he held the car door open and guided her inside before closing it behind her and rounding the hood. Jesus, he would never be able to drive the Jaguar again and not think of what happened on top of it today. And the fact that a smile eased onto his face at the thought should've alarmed him. Maybe when his body wasn't loose and relaxed after the best sex he ever had, it would.

His cell phone rang as he slid behind the steering wheel. Silently groaning, he reached for it. Damn. He'd forgotten that he'd powered his phone back on a couple of hours ago for the first time since leaving for Vegas. Yes, he'd been out of the office and unavailable for longer than, well, ever, but he wasn't ready to face everything head-on yet. He glanced at the screen, intending to note the caller ID and then send the call to voice mail. But when his brother's name popped up, he hesitated.

It was Luke. And he was most likely worried.

Shit.

Swiping the answer bar, Ezekiel lifted the phone to his ear. "Hey, Luke."

"Where the hell have you been?" his brother roared.

Pinching the bridge of his nose, he glanced over at Reagan to find her studying him, eyebrows arched.

"Vegas. I instructed Laura to let everyone know I would be out of town and to reschedule anything that came up," he said calmly. "I'm a married man, by the way."

"Congratulations," Luke said, even if it seemed to emerge through gritted teeth. "But Laura said a couple of days, not four."

"Yes, I took two more days," Ezekiel ground out, trying not to snap. "What's the big damn deal, Luke? Yes, we're in trouble, but the company isn't going to collapse while I take some vacation time."

Silence greeted his outburst.

An ominous silence that sent dread crawling down his spine. "Luke?" His grip on his cell tightened until the case bit into his palm. "What's going on? What's wrong?"

A heavy sigh echoed down the line. "I'm sorry, Zeke. Sorry for coming at you like I did." Luke paused, and because they were so in tune with each other, Ezekiel could easily imagine his brother scrubbing a hand over his head in frustration. "And wish I could've called you with better news when you just returned from your honeymoon, but... Zeke, the shit has hit the fan."

"What?" Ezekiel snarled, his heart pounding so loud against his chest he could barely hear his brother above the din. "Dammit, tell me, Luke."

"With our assets frozen, the company hasn't been able to cover debts. One of them being the estate." Luke's voice thickened, and Ezekiel's throat closed in response. "Zeke, the bank foreclosed on our home. Everyone's been forced to move out. Harley is living with Grant until their move back to Thailand. Beth's gone to live with Camden. Sebastian and Sutton are renting a house together, and I'm crashing with a friend for now. But Aunt Ava..." Again Luke paused, and his dark rumble of anger reverberated in Ezekiel's ear. "She's moved in with Keith."

"Goddammit," Ezekiel snarled. Out of his peripheral vision, he caught Reagan's head snapping toward him. Her arm stretched across the console and she clasped his free hand in hers. "He's taking advantage of her, Luke, and using the situation to get her under his thumb. Just when we were starting to get her back to her old self after Uncle Trent's death. Now she's..." He trailed off, squeezing his eyes closed. "How is this all happening?" he whispered. "Why is this..."

"I don't know, Zeke," came his brother's solemn answer. "I really don't."

Fourteen

"Reagan, can I just say again how much I appreciate you agreeing to help with the masquerade ball?" Her pretty green eyes shining, Beth Wingate reached across the table in the small meeting room in the Texas Cattleman's Clubhouse and squeezed Reagan's hand. "Especially since Zeke volunteered you without asking first. I hope you know I warned my cousin against making that a habit in your marriage," she drawled.

Reagan laughed, waving away the other woman's concern. "It's no problem at all, really. With Dad being a member of the club for so long, I'm no stranger to helping out with the events they've sponsored. Honestly, I'm happy to help out in any way I can."

"Good, I'm glad." Beth gave Reagan's hand one last squeeze. "And since I haven't yet had the opportunity to congratulate you on your new marriage, congratulations." Her smile dimmed a little, shadows entering her eyes. "I know this wasn't the homecoming you were expecting though. And I'm sorry you had to return to this…mess."

Reagan didn't have to ask to what *mess* Beth referred. Until two weeks ago, the oldest Wingate daughter had been living on the estate with her family. But now she resided with her fiancé, Camden Guthrie, due to the foreclosure on the family properties.

Beth, lovely and elegant with a slim build and dark blond hair, had always been the epitome of composure and grace. But even she appeared a little tired and strained despite reuniting months ago with her first love. The trials the family faced obviously weighed on her. And having to continue to organize the TCC's charity masquerade must be one more added pressure.

"The masquerade ball is next month, in October, and even though a few people have regrettably returned their tickets because of our…association with the event, ticket sales are still steady. At least most folks are more interested in attending the social event of the year than in shunning the Wingates." Beth's mouth straightened into a grim line before she shook her head. "Anyway, I really hate that our family issues are overshadowing your marriage, Reagan."

"Please don't apologize, Beth. Our vows included 'for better or worse.' We're just experiencing a bit of the worse right now." Reagan shrugged a shoulder, the relaxed gesture belying the tangle of knots in her stomach. "Besides, it's not like we have the most conventional of marriages."

"Do any of us?" Harley chimed in from next to her. Her childhood friend tipped her head to the side, her long, straight brown hair falling over her shoulder as she studied Reagan. "I mean, Beth reunited with her long-lost love after a ton of lies and secrets. I had a whole secret baby scandal. But the point is we ended up with the men we love and who love us in return."

"Isn't that just like happy couples? You're in love so you see it everywhere." Reagan huffed a chuckle. As delighted as she was to have her old friend back in Royal after five years—even if it was only until after her upcoming wedding—she'd forgotten about Harley's stubbornness. "I adore you like a sister, Harley, but I don't want you to start making Zeke and me into the next fairy tale. We married so I could receive my inheritance, that's all." Even though that goal didn't look obtainable at the moment.

Harley waved away Reagan's objection. "I know, I know, that's the party line between you and Zeke. Regardless of the hows and whys, I'm just glad my best friend and my cousin are together. You make a great couple. And I believe you're good for each other."

Before Reagan could reply, Gracie Diaz swept into the meeting room. "Hey, everyone. I'm so sorry I'm late," she said, the apology slightly breathless.

Reagan remembered Gracie Diaz from her time spent at the Wingate estate. Only a couple of years older than her, Gracie had been the daughter of a family ranch hand, and later, hired by Beth as an assistant for the various charities she managed. Even though there'd been a difference in their statuses, she and Beth were very good friends. But more recently, Gracie had become a national celebrity for winning the sixty-million-dollar Powerball lottery. She was Royal's own rags-to-riches story.

As the stunning brunette pulled out one of the chairs and sat—no, collapsed—onto it, Reagan narrowed her eyes, studying her. Nothing could detract from the beauty of Gracie's thick, dark hair and lovely brown eyes, but Reagan still couldn't help but notice the faint circles under slightly puffy eyes, as if she'd recently been crying.

"No problem, Gracie." Beth frowned, scooting to the edge of her seat and wrapping an arm around her friend's shoulders. Pulling her close for a quick hug, she said, "Now don't take this the wrong way, hon, but you look terrible." Gracie snorted, and Beth grinned at the other woman. "The masquerade plans can wait. What's going on?"

Gracie propped her elbows on the table and pressed her palms to her forehead. "I swear, since winning the lottery and all that money, I've vacillated between being eternally thankful and cursing the day my numbers pulled up." She sighed, and the sound contained so much exhaustion, Reagan winced in sympathy. "Growing up, I never did understand the saying *more money, more problems*, because we never had money. But now…"

"Gracie, what's happened?" Harley pressed, leaning forward and clasping her upper arm.

"You must not have seen the news today," Gracie said, tunneling her fingers through her hair, then dragging the thick strands away from her face. "Apparently my cousin is claiming he bought the lottery ticket, and I stole it from him. Now he's insisting I turn more than half the winnings over to him. Which is ridiculous. I haven't seen my uncle's son in years, but now suddenly I'm a thief who steals from family."

Reagan snatched her phone from her purse, and in moments, brought up the local news' website and viewed the clip posted at the top of the home page. Apparently Gracie's family drama had temporarily replaced the Wingates as the newest scandal. Silently, she watched as a reporter interviewed Alberto Diaz outside Royal's town hall. He claimed that he was devastated and angry that his own cousin could betray him. Convincing sorrow etched his features as he gave his forgiveness to Gracie, but still demanded half of the money.

The sound bite skipped to the same reporter racing to reach Gracie as she opened her car door. Understandably, Gracie was angry at the accusation and refuted the lie before ducking into her car and driving off.

"He's lying," Reagan declared, dropping her phone onto the table.

"Of course he is," Harley agreed fiercely, her eyes blazing. "I can't believe they even gave him airtime for that. They're no better than a tabloid spreading that garbage."

"Yes, well, unfortunately, people thrive on that kind of trash. And it's easier for them to believe the salacious things than the truth." Gracie lifted her hands, palms up. "I'm sorry. I didn't mean to unload this on all of you. There's nothing I can do about it right now."

"You're going to fight him, aren't you?" Beth demanded.

"Oh, you're damn right," Gracie seethed. "I don't mind helping family out. I'm buying Mom a new home in Florida so she can be closer to her sister, and I'm paying for my brother to attend a private school so he can achieve every one of his dreams. So, if Alberto would've asked me for help, for money, I would've gladly given it to him. But this? Accusing me of a crime and trying to extort half of my winnings? That's blackmail, and I'm not giving in to it."

"Good for you!" Reagan praised, admiring this woman's grit and backbone. "And if there's anything we can do, just let us know. You got us in your corner ready to fight."

For the first time since she entered the room, Gracie smiled. "Thank you, Reagan. All of you." She pressed her palms to the tabletop. "Okay, enough about my unscrupulous family woes. Where are we with the masquerade ball?"

Beth covered her friend's hand and squeezed before picking up a paper and passing it to Harley. "I was just about to tell Harley and Reagan about the Cinderella Sweepstakes."

"Anything with Cinderella in it, I'm for it," Reagan teased, accepting the sheet Harley held out to her.

"I know, right?" Beth grinned. "You have the details there, but the gist of it is the local radio station offered a free makeover and ticket to one lucky winner. And considering each ticket is a thousand dollars, this is a wonderful opportunity. The station came up with the name Cinderella Sweepstakes. Isn't that perfect? The contest should bring more publicity and money to the ball. Fingers crossed. With all of us working together, it's going to be a wonderful success this year."

The meeting continued for the next couple of hours, and by the time Reagan left the clubhouse and pulled up outside the small town house rental she and Ezekiel had moved into, satisfaction was a warm glow inside of her. Satisfaction and excitement.

Working with the Wingate women and Gracie had stirred ideas about a possible fundraiser for the girls' home where she volunteered. With her father withholding her inheritance, Reagan might not be able to build her own home anytime soon, but that didn't mean she couldn't come up with an alternative to support the unwed and pregnant girls who needed help. And that included investing her time.

But with Ezekiel and his family feverishly working to salvage what was left of Wingate Enterprises, that time might be reduced as she needed to look for a job. She refused to just stand by while her husband exhausted himself to support her.

An agenda other than love might've been behind their marriage, but she meant what she'd told Beth earlier. For better or worse. And though their union had a time limit, she would stand beside him for however long she wore his last name.

Longer.

Climbing from the car, she shut the door behind her and strode up the short walk to the front door.

"Reagan," someone called behind her.

Lowering the key she'd been about to slide into the door, Reagan turned and smiled as Piper Holloway, Ezekiel's aunt, approached her, carrying a large brown-paper-covered parcel.

"Here, let me get that for you," Reagan said, hurrying toward the other woman.

But Piper laughed. "No need. I'm fine. Believe me, running an art gallery as many years as I have has given me muscles you probably can't see." Reaching Reagan, she leaned over and brushed an airy kiss over her cheek. "I have a little housewarming gift for you and my sneaky nephew." She tsked, shaking her head. "Running off to get married without a word to any of us. If I wasn't so happy for both of you, I'd be more than a little upset I didn't get to stand beside you two on your wedding day."

"It was a little spur-of-the-moment, otherwise I know he would've wanted you there," Reagan murmured. It was true. While Ava Wingate could be a little standoffish, her younger sister Piper was incredibly open and warm. Harley, at least, had preferred her aunt's company and easy affection to her mother's frequent criticism. "And thank you for the gift. You didn't have to travel all the way from Dallas to bring it."

"My pleasure. I wanted to congratulate you two in person anyway."

"Well, I know Zeke will be pleased to see you," Reagan said, turning back to the door and unlocking it. "Come on in."

She stepped back and allowed Piper to enter first. "Hey, Zeke, I'm back," Reagan announced, shutting the door behind her. "Look who I found outside—" She drew to a halt, spying that Ezekiel wasn't alone. "Oh, I'm sorry. I didn't know you had company."

"Hey, sweetheart," Ezekiel greeted, striding forward. He pressed a quick kiss to her lips, then, removing the package from his aunt's grasp, drew her in for a one-armed hug. Reagan's lips tingled, and she forced herself not to touch them. *Part of the show*, she reminded herself. *It's all for show.* "Aunt Piper, I didn't know you were coming over."

"I'm that impolite guest that just drops by unannounced," she joked, wrapping an arm around her nephew's waist and squeezing.

Ezekiel chuckled. "Never impolite or unwelcome. Have you met Brian Cooper?" He turned toward the tall, dark-haired man standing next to the living room couch. "Reagan, Aunt Piper, this is Brian Cooper, an attorney from the Dallas area. His uncle is Keith Cooper."

Surprise winged through Reagan at that bit of news. Why would Keith's nephew be here at their home? Especially considering how Ezekiel felt about the man his aunt Ava had moved in with.

"Brian," Ezekiel went on, "I'd like to introduce you to my wife, Reagan, and my aunt, Piper Holloway."

"It's nice to meet you both." Brian crossed the small room and shook hands with both of them.

Although, his gaze lingered on Piper.

O-kay.

With sharpened interest, Reagan studied the other man and woman. Piper, slim, tall, with her edgy, short cut and dark green eyes, was an older, beautiful, sophisticated woman. And apparently Brian, who couldn't look away from her, seemed to agree. They did make a striking couple. And from the way Piper tried—and failed—not to study the younger man from under her dark lashes, she had to notice how handsome the attorney with the athletic build was.

As if he could sense her thoughts, Brian glanced at her, and Reagan arched an eyebrow, a smile tugging at the corner of her mouth. "So you're from Dallas, too?" she asked. "Piper owns one of the most influential and prestigious art galleries there."

"Holloway Gallery downtown?" Brian asked Piper.

"Yes, that's me," Piper acknowledged. "Have you been in before?"

"Yes, I've been to a couple of shows there." He slid

his hands into the front pockets of his pants. "The gallery isn't far from my office. Maybe we could get together for a cup of coffee soon."

"We'll see," she murmured, then switched her attention to her nephew. "Since I didn't get an invite to the wedding—and don't think I'm letting you off the hook for that anytime soon—I brought by a painting for your new home."

The next half hour flew by, and when Piper and Brian left, Reagan closed the door behind them, then whipped around to face Ezekiel.

"I think your friend has a crush on your aunt," she teased.

He snorted. "I hate it for him if he does, because even I felt that brush-off."

"Yeah, it was kind of obvious. Why do you think she did? Piper tried to hide it, but she kept peeking at him." Reagan frowned. "You think maybe she's self-conscious about the age difference? Which is silly. He is younger, but she's a gorgeous, vivacious and successful woman. Any man, regardless of age, would be lucky to have her look their way."

"Sweetheart, are you really asking me to think about my aunt's dating habits? As far as I'm concerned, she's a virgin," Ezekiel drawled.

Laughing, Reagan strode across the floor to him. After a brief hesitation, she pressed against him and circled her arms around his neck. Rising to her toes, she kissed him, and the desire that never banked for him flickered into higher, hotter flames.

They hadn't drawn up rules dictating this new turn in their relationship. Part of her was okay with it— no rules meant she couldn't break them when she just wanted to casually touch him like this. But the other part of her needed to know what they were doing. Because every time she kissed him, touched him, woke up next to him, she couldn't stop craving more. Even if her mind warned her against that greed, that it could only end in heartache, her heart didn't seem to be heeding the memo.

Because somewhere along the line, her heart had chosen him. Maybe when she'd come upon him visiting his ex-fiancée's grave. Maybe when he'd laid his head in her lap and allowed her to help ease some of his burden. Maybe when he hadn't judged her after she'd revealed her past.

Did it really matter when? Her stupid, never-learn-its-damn-lesson heart had thrown itself at him, and he was Teflon. At sixteen, her reckless, headfirst dive into love could be chalked up to immaturity. But this dizzying, terrifying leap? She was going in knowing Ezekiel didn't want her future, her affection outside of the bedroom, and most certainly not her love.

And yet…

Yet he had it. All of her.

"How was your day?" Ezekiel asked, planting one last kiss against her mouth.

"Good." She forced a smile to her lips even though it trembled. "I spent time at the girls' home, then headed over to the clubhouse for a meeting with Beth, Harley and Gracie about the masquerade ball. I bought tickets for us, by the way. I wanted to get ours before they were sold out—what? What's wrong?"

"Nothing. Go ahead with what you were saying." Ezekiel shrugged, stepping back and heading out of the small foyer toward the living room.

No, she hadn't imagined that flicker of unease in his eyes or the tightening of his mouth. Something had triggered his reaction. Running her words through her head, she stared at his back and the tense set of his wide shoulders.

"Zeke, if it's about the tickets... If you'd prefer not to attend the ball because of everything that's going on, I fully understand. It's just that the rest of your family is going, and I thought you'd want to be there as well. But I can—"

"Ray," he said, voice soft but firm. "We're going to the ball. Please drop it. Everything's fine."

No. Everything *wasn't* fine, but he wouldn't share with her. Since returning from Vegas, Ezekiel had grown increasingly distant. Not physically—he was as passionate and insatiable with her as ever. Even more so in some ways. As if an element of desperation had crept into the sex. But a wall had sprung up around his emotions. Like now. He stood mere feet away from her, but he might as well as be on the other side of Royal. Or at the office, where he spent hours and hours into the night trying to salvage his family's business.

Speaking of...

"What are you doing home so early?" she asked. "It's only six, and usually you're still at the office. Did something happen?"

He shook his head, a faint smile playing at the corner of his sensual lips. "No, sweetheart. Everything's fine. I just asked Brian to meet me here instead of at the office. I wanted to talk with him about the legal issues with your inheritance. And I didn't want to do that at the office."

"I wondered about that. Are you sure you can trust him? I know how you feel about his uncle."

Ezekiel rubbed his bearded jaw. "I really like him in spite of who he's related to. I've met him before, and he's always struck me as a good guy. And a damn good attorney. He promised to look into your grandmother's will and see if there's a way to get around your father's hold on your inheritance."

"That's good," she said. "Do you think maybe you could ask him to look into something else as well?" She relayed the circumstances around Gracie and her cousin. "Maybe knowing what legal claim her cousin actually has will give her some ammunition going into this battle."

"Damn, I hate that for Gracie. This money should be a blessing, not a curse." Ezekiel pulled his cell phone from his pants pocket, then tapped out something on the screen. "I have something even better. I'll ask Miles if he can find out anything on this cousin. If he isn't able to, then it can't be found."

Miles Wingate, Ezekiel's cousin, owned Steel Security, a company that protected high-powered clients both physically and online. No doubt he could unearth any information on Alberto Diaz.

"Thanks, Zeke. I'm sure Gracie would appreciate it."

"She's family," he said simply, and for him, that was it. Family took care of family.

"Oh, I have some potentially good news," Reagan announced, circling around Ezekiel and picking up the coffee cups and saucers on the table in front of the couch. "I let the supervisor over at the home know that I would be cutting back on my volunteer time since I would be looking for employment. And she said an administrative position might be opening with the organization, and she would put my name in for it. With my experience there, she thinks I would be a good fit. So not only would I have a job but at a place I love."

"That's wonderful, sweetheart," he murmured. "I hope it works out."

There it was again. That note in his voice. That flash of emotion across his face and in his eyes.

"Zeke," she said, the cups and plates suddenly weighing down her arms.

"Reagan." He stepped closer, cradling her face and tilting his head down. He placed a tender kiss on her forehead, then nudged her chin up to look into her eyes. "Seriously, with your passion for their project, they would be fools not to snatch you up." He took the cups and saucers from her. "How about going out for dinner tonight?"

With a kiss to her temple, he left the living room for the kitchen, leaving her to stare behind him.

He couldn't fool her. Something *was* bothering him.

But why didn't he share it with her? What was he *not* telling her?

And why did the thought of it have unease curdling in her stomach?

Fifteen

Ezekiel sipped from his glass of whiskey as he stared out the dark window of his new living room. This late at night, he couldn't see much, but he knew what lay beyond the glass. And the view of the tiny, fenced-in backyard with its postage-stamp-size patio couldn't be more different than the rolling, green hills of the ranch where he'd lived for so many years.

I would be cutting back on my volunteer time since I would be looking for employment.

I bought tickets for us, by the way.

He lifted an arm, pressed a palm to the wall and bowed his head. But that did nothing but amplify the words ricocheting in his head. *Dammit.* Straightening, he tipped his glass back and downed the rest of the alcohol. As it blazed a path down his throat, he welcomed the burn when it hit his chest. Anything was better than the dread and hated sense of inevitability that usually resided there these days.

God knows, he wasn't one of those men who preferred that their women not work. They needed to feel fulfilled and purposeful, too. But that wasn't why Reagan was seeking a job. *He* was the reason. The scandal and the resulting fallout that threatened his family's company and reputation and his own investments. They were living off his savings right now, and they weren't anywhere near the poorhouse, but to Reagan…

He huffed out a hard, ragged breath.

Her father had been right. Ezekiel might be able to provide for her, but he couldn't protect her from the whispers, the condemnation, the scorn. He'd married her so she could have freedom and all he'd given her was a prison sentence to a man and family scarred by scandal. He'd failed her in every way that counted. At least to him as a man, a husband. Hell, he'd had to call another man and ask him for help to solve his wife's problem. Because he couldn't do it himself.

Just today, they'd had to lay off more employees from Wingate. Employees who depended on him, on his family, for their livelihoods. And all he could do was sit in his office with his thumb up his ass futilely trying to figure out a way to help. To do fucking *something*.

If he couldn't save his family's company, how could he possibly help Reagan save her inheritance, help her achieve her dream of a home for unwed, pregnant teens here in Royal? Help her have the life, the future she wanted?

The answer was simple.

He couldn't.

He'd failed Melissa so many years ago. He'd failed the Wingates.

He'd failed Reagan.

And with her beautiful, wounded heart, her indomitable spirit and strength, she deserved better. So much better.

Better was a man who could protect her from the ugliness of life and follow through on his promises.

Better was a man who was brave enough to love her without fear.

Better was not him.

"Zeke?"

Lowering his arm, he pivoted to find Reagan standing in the hall entrance, a black nightgown molding to her sensual curves. The sucker punch of desire to his gut wasn't a surprise. By now, he accepted that he wouldn't be able to look at her, to be in the same damn state as her, and not want her.

He turned back to the window.

"What're you doing up, Reagan?" He'd waited until she'd fallen asleep, their skin still damp from sex, before he'd left their bed.

"I should ask you that same question. And I am. What's wrong, Zeke?" Moments later, her fingers curled around the hand still holding the empty tumbler. She gently took it from him, setting it on the table behind them. "And don't tell me nothing again. I can see how stressed you are. How tired. It's Wingate, isn't it?"

He didn't immediately reply, mentally corralling and organizing his words. But when he parted his lips, nothing of the pat, simple reply emerged.

"When I told Luke about our engagement, he accused me of trying to save you. Because I failed with Melissa."

"Failed with Melissa?" she repeated. "Zeke, she died in a car accident."

"Yes." He nodded, images of that night so long ago flashing across the screen of his mind. "But what you don't know is I was supposed to be in the car that night. I was supposed to be driving. If I had been, maybe…" He didn't finish the thought, but he didn't need to. He'd repeated the words so often over the years, they were engraved on his soul.

"Then maybe you would both be dead," Reagan said, grasping his upper arm and tugging until he turned from the window and looked down at her.

Dammit. He hadn't wanted to do that. Would've avoided staring down into her beautiful face if he had his way. Because those espresso eyes, elegant cheekbones and lush mouth unraveled his already frayed resolve.

"There is no guarantee that you would've been able to save her. The only person responsible for her death is the drunk driver who crashed into her. This isn't your burden to bear, Zeke."

He heard her—had heard the same from Luke, Harley and Piper over the years. But the guilt remained. It burrowed down deep below bone and marrow.

"You know, when I first told Luke I asked you to marry me, he accused me of having a savior complex—of trying to rescue you, because I couldn't do the same with Melissa. I told Luke that wasn't true," he continued, not addressing her assertion of his innocence. "And at the time, I believed it. Melissa had nothing to do with you, and I wasn't trying to save you. But now…" He gently removed her hand from his arm. "Now, I think he had a point, and I was fooling myself into believing I could help you. Provide for you. *Protect* you. I can't, Reagan. Your father was right, and we both know it."

Shock blanked her eyes and parted her lips. Her soft gasp echoed in the room, and he locked his arms at his sides to keep from wrapping her in them. When he'd suggested this arrangement those months ago, his goal had been to avoid the pain that gleamed in her gaze. But now, to be the cause of it... He closed his eyes, yet seconds later reopened them. He did this; it would be a coward's move not to face it.

"When I asked you to marry me—when you agreed—this wasn't the life you envisioned, and it wasn't the one I promised you. Your father said I couldn't take care of you, that I would only bring you hardship and scandal, and he was right. I took away the life you've known, the one you deserve. Because of me, you're estranged from your family and still don't have access to your inheritance."

"You don't know what you're saying, Zeke."

"Yes...I do," he ground out. "I failed you, Reagan, and all I can offer you now to make it right is a divorce. Then you can have your relationship back with your parents and a chance at the money your grandmother wanted you to have. You can have your dreams and the girls' home you were meant to build. I refuse to take all that away from you."

"Am I so easy to toss aside, Zeke?" she whispered, her fingers lifting to that scar on her collarbone.

"Ray, no," he murmured. Nothing about this was easy. It was ripping him to shreds inside. "That's not true." He reached for her, to draw her hand away from that mark that represented so much tragedy for her, but she stumbled back, away from his touch.

"My ex. My parents. You. What is it about me that's so easy for people to walk away from?" She paced away from him, dragging fingers through her hair. Her hollow burst of laughter reverberated in the room. "No, I take that back. This isn't on me. It wasn't ever on me," she said softly, almost as if to herself.

Spinning around, she faced him again, and he was almost rocked back on his heels by her beauty and the fury in her eyes. "For too long I've blamed myself for whatever deficit in me permitted people to abandon me. I'm through with that. And you don't get to use me as an excuse for running scared and not owning your own shit."

"What do you think I'm doing now, dammit?" He took a step toward her before drawing to an abrupt halt. "Do you think it's easy for me to admit that I've failed you? That I couldn't give you everything I promised? That I wasn't—"

He bit off the rest of that statement, hating to think it much less state it aloud. But she didn't have that problem.

"*Enough?* You weren't enough to save Melissa. You aren't enough to save Wingate. And you aren't enough to save me?" For a moment, her expression softened, but then it hardened into an icy mask. One he hadn't seen on her before tonight. "News flash, Zeke. I didn't ask you to. It isn't me you're so concerned with protecting—it's yourself. I threaten that pain and guilt that you've become so comfortable carrying around it's now a part of you. Because to admit that I'm more than a charity case to you means you would have to deal with the reality that you stand in your own way of finding acceptance and love. You'll have to face the truth that you've been lonely and alone out of choice, not cruel fate."

Anger sparked inside him, flicking high and hot. As did fear. But he fanned the flames of his anger, smoking out that other, weaker emotion. He wasn't *afraid*. She didn't know him. Didn't know all he'd suffered, lost. How could he not throw up shields around his heart? To protect himself from that kind of devastation? Even now, knowing he was letting her go, damn near pushing her out the door, had pain pumping through his veins instead of blood. But the thought of how much worse it would be if something happened to her...

No. Fuck it. Call him a coward. Selfish.

He couldn't do it. Not again.

"Zeke."

He dragged his gaze from the floor and returned it to her face.

The fury that saturated her features thawed, leaving behind a sadness that cut just as deep as her hurt. She sighed, shaking her head. "You *are* enough. You're more than enough. But I can't make you believe or accept it, so I'm leaving. Not because of some perceived stink of association with you. I'm leaving because the first time you 'released' me for my own good, I let you. Then I returned and begged you to marry me. I won't do it again, and I won't stay with a man who doesn't want me enough to fight for me. For us. And I damn sure won't beg him to let me stay."

She strode forward and past him. He lifted an arm in a belated attempt to reach for her, to try to make her understand why he was a bad bet. Why he was putting her before his wants and needs. Because she was wrong—he did want her. Too much.

But either she didn't see his hand or she didn't want his touch, because she blew past him and headed toward the hall leading to their bedroom. He parted his lips to call after her, but then she stopped in the opening without turning around, her slim back straight, her shoulders drawn back.

"I didn't need you to be my superhero. I am fully capable of saving myself. I needed you to be my friend, my lover, my husband. I needed you to love me more than your fear of opening your heart up again. Just like I love you more than my fear of being abandoned again. And for the record, you were—you *are*—worth the risk. But this time? I'm walking away. Because I'm worth the risk, too."

Then she walked away. Just like she'd promised.

Sixteen

Reagan climbed the steps to her parents' home and, twisting the knob, pushed the front door open. Since her mother was expecting her for lunch, there was no need to knock.

Standing in the quiet foyer, she surveyed it as if she hadn't been there in years instead of weeks. Since that confrontation with her father, she hadn't stepped foot in the home that had been hers since birth. The only reason she did so now was because of a phone call from her mother, asking her to please come over so they could talk. The *I miss you* at the end had sealed Reagan's fate. It was difficult to tell Henrietta Sinclair no on the best of terms. But when she tacked on the emotional warfare? Impossible.

The familiar scent of lemon and roses enveloped her, as comforting as a hug. Funny to think there'd been a time when she'd hated the scent of roses. But now? Now she missed it as much as she missed her family.

Especially now, when she didn't have anyone.

Well, that wasn't exactly true. She had Harley, who was graciously letting her stay with her and Grant until her new apartment came available next week. She had Beth and Gracie, who had been so saddened when she'd told them a week ago about the breakup with Zeke. But had quickly assured her she was still family to them.

And of course, and most important, she had herself.

That night with Ezekiel had been a revelation of sorts. A revelation that though her past might have shaped the woman she'd become, she was not the sum of her mistakes. Just as she'd told Zeke, she didn't need saving; she wasn't some damsel in distress. And her dream of a girls' home here in Royal wouldn't crumble to dust just because her father held her inheritance hostage. Her dream hadn't been birthed by either her father or Ezekiel, so neither one could—or would—be the death of it.

She loved him... *God*, did she love him. That love was rooted in friendship, admiration, respect and a desire that even now her soul-deep hurt hadn't banished. But she valued who she was and what she brought to the table of their marriage more. That he couldn't see how she possessed the strength to carry him just as he did her... She shook her head. Maybe it was good their relationship ended when it did. That lack of regard for her would've surely poisoned them long before he decided the expiration date on their arrangement had come due.

Inhaling a breath, she shoved away those thoughts and the pain they resonated through her body for the time being.

"Mom?" she called, walking toward the rear of the house and the smaller salon her mother usually occupied this time of day, working on her numerous charitable events and committee responsibilities.

"In here, Reagan."

That was *not* her mother. Shock ricocheted through her like a Ping-Pong ball, and she skidded to a stop on her heels, frozen. After several moments, she unglued her feet and reversed course toward the formal living room. She'd heard her father's voice but seeing him standing there in the middle of the room pelted her with more icy shards of surprise.

"Dad," she said, amazed her voice remained calm when inside she was the exact opposite. "What are you doing here? I was supposed to meet Mom for lunch."

He cleared his throat and locked his hands behind his back. And oh, how she'd missed him. Reserved, domineering and often stern to the point of being implacable. But he was also protective, loving in his own way and willing to lay down his life for his family. They were all what defined Douglas Sinclair, and the distance between them had left a hollow, empty place in her heart.

"I apologize for the deception, but I asked her to arrange this..." he waved a hand between them "...meeting. Otherwise, I didn't know if you would agree to come."

It was on the tip of her tongue to say she would've, but at the last moment, she swallowed the words. Because she might not have, given that it might've meant subjecting herself to another blistering lecture.

"Well, I'm here now," she said, moving farther into the room. "What's going on, Dad?"

Instead of answering, he reached inside his suit jacket and removed an envelope. He crossed the short distance separating them and handed it to her. She tore her gaze away from him and glanced down at the piece of mail.

"Please," he insisted. "Open it."

With a frown, she acquiesced. And minutes later, the paper trembled in her shaking hand. Unsure that she could've read the single sheet correctly, she scanned it again. But no, the terms remained the same. Her grandmother's inheritance had been released to her.

He'd released it to her.

"Dad," she breathed, stunned at the enormity of this. But then an ugly idea crept into her mind, and she lowered the paper to her side. "Is this because I left Zeke?" she demanded. "Because I don't want to be 'rewarded' for that. It had nothing to do with—"

"No, Reagan," Douglas interrupted her. "It has nothing to do with that. I'd decided to give you the inheritance a couple of weeks ago. It's just taken me this long to get past my pride to speak to you." He sighed, and once again, astonishment paralyzed her. Outward displays of emotion—sadness, pain, regret, which he usually kept so sternly in check—softened his eyes and turned his mouth down at the corners. Her heart thudded against her sternum. "The love a parent has for their child…" He shook his head. "It's so hard to explain, but I want to try."

He paced to the large fireplace and silently studied its dark depths before turning back to her. And though his familiar, serious expression was firmly in place once more, his voice shook with the feelings she'd spied only seconds ago.

"Being black in Texas was…rough for your mother and me. Especially in the time we came of age in. And infiltrating the business world carried its own set of hindrances and injustices. But for you, your brother and sister and mother, I would endure it all again. You all are worth every ugly name, every snub, every racist hurdle I had to climb or break through. Still, I swore to myself my children would never have to suffer that kind of pain, struggle and discrimination. I wanted better for you…because I love you so much.

"I guess you could call it an obsession of mine—making sure you were all right. Especially after the pregnancy when you were sixteen. I felt so…helpless. My baby girl was hurting, had been taken advantage of, and I felt like I'd failed in protecting you. And I know I didn't handle the situation right. I don't regret paying off that boy because he was no good for you, but I do regret that in the middle of my pain and powerlessness I made you feel like I didn't love you anymore. That somehow you were less in my eyes. When in truth, I wanted to wrap you up and shield you more."

He paused, then shifted, his profile facing her as he stared out the huge picture window. The view of Pine Valley was lovely, but she doubted he saw it. And she couldn't focus on anything but her father and the words that both hurt and healed.

"Since I failed in protecting you—"

"Dad, that's just not true," Reagan objected fiercely.

He shook his head, holding up a hand. "To me, I didn't do my job as your father. All I wanted for you was a life where you didn't experience that ever again. If something should happen to me tomorrow, I wouldn't have to worry because I'd know you were taken of.

Which, for me, meant a husband who could provide for you, care for you, insulate you with his name, his wealth and connections so you wouldn't ever know being poor, disdained or abandoned. Never know mistreatment or mishandling of your precious heart again.

"But nearly losing you because of my own agenda and shortsightedness revealed to me that I took it too far. I was so concerned with you being hurt by society, by this world, that I ended up being the one who hurt you. In my drive to protect you out of love, I forgot compassion. Understanding. Forgiveness. Mercy. All of those are elements of the love I touted. I also forgot that struggle often shapes a person, makes them stronger. It helps us be better. And while I detest what you went through, it did make you into a better, stronger person, and…" He shifted back to her and tears glistened in his eyes. "I love you. And I'm proud of you."

He lifted his arms, slowly opening them to her, and without hesitation she flew into them.

And in that moment, as her arms wrapped around his waist, her cheek pressed to his chest, the sixteen-year-old girl and the adult woman converged into one. "I love you, too, Dad."

Seventeen

"What the hell?" Ezekiel stared at the email from his personal accountant. More specifically, the numbers inside the email. There were a shit ton of zeroes in that number. "This can't be…"

But even as he murmured the objection, he re-read the message again, and there it was in black and white.

He was a millionaire.

For the first time since Reagan walked away from him and out of his house, he felt something other than a pain-infused grief. Like a death. Only difference, there wasn't a tombstone to visit.

You did the right thing. The only thing you could do.

He repeated the reminder that had become a refrain in his head over the last week. Whenever he teetered on the edge of giving in, yelling, "Fuck this," and going after her, he remembered that he was doing what was best for her.

Best for you.

The taunt whispered across his mind, and he flipped that voice a mental bird.

"What can't be?" a familiar and unexpected voice asked.

Ezekiel jerked his head up and watched Luke close Ezekiel's office door behind him and cross the floor to his desk. Even though the workday was only a couple of hours old, Luke had rolled the sleeves of his dress shirt to his elbows, undone the top button, and his tie knot was loosened.

Concern momentarily overshadowed Ezekiel's shock. No one in this company was working harder than Luke to save it. And it showed in the faint bruises under his brother's eyes denoting lack of sleep, the hollowed cheekbones and firm lines bracketing his mouth.

"When was the last time you went home and had a decent night's sleep?" Ezekiel demanded.

Luke dismissed his question with a flick of his hand. "What can't be?" he repeated. "You receive some good news?"

"Yes," Ezekiel said, struggling against badgering Luke into answering his question. Shaking his head, he shifted his attention from his brother's weary features to the computer screen and the open email. "I just received a message from my accountant." He huffed out a breath, disbelief coursing through him once more. "I have a few personal investments outside of Wingate and apparently, one of the companies I invested in just sold for billions. Billions, Luke. And I'm a millionaire because of it."

Joy lit up his brother's light brown eyes, eclipsing the exhaustion there.

"Holy shit, Zeke!" Luke grinned, rounding the desk to pull Ezekiel up out of his chair and jerk him into a back-pounding hug. "That's wonderful. Damn, I'm glad we finally have some good news around here."

"I'm still in shock. I don't even know what to do right now," Ezekiel murmured.

"I do. Go get Reagan back."

Ezekiel's chin jerked up and back from Luke's verbal sucker punch. "What?" Just hearing her name… It scored him, leaving red-hot slashes of pain behind. "What the hell are you talking about?"

"I'm talking about going to find your wife, get down on your knees if need be and beg her to come back to you," Luke stated flatly. "I love you, Zeke, but you fucked up."

A growl vibrated in his chest, rolling up into his throat, but at the last moment, he didn't let his angry retort fly. Luke loved him and meant well. But still… Ezekiel didn't want to hear this. "Luke, I appreciate—"

"No," Luke interjected with a hard shake of his head. "You're my brother and the most important person in the world to me. Which is why I can tell you the brutal truth even though you don't want to hear it. And I can do it knowing it won't hurt our relationship."

Ezekiel almost turned away, but only his love for his brother kept him from walking away. Well, that, and he harbored zero doubts Luke would drag him back to make him listen.

Luke sighed, rubbing a hand over the back of his neck. "I know I warned you against marrying Reagan when you first told me about the engagement. I was worried for both of you. But when I saw you two at the engagement party, I changed my mind. You belong together... You belong *to* her. And I say this remembering how you were with Melissa. I loved her—she was sweet, kind and loved you. But Melissa is gone, and you have the chance for a future with a woman who not only fiercely defended you like a lioness but who challenges you. Who makes you better. Who loves you. And you, whether you want to admit it to yourself or not, love her."

"Love?" Ezekiel laughed, and the serrated edge of it scraped his throat. "You say that when we have so many examples around us of people who have been gutted by love. Like when you love someone, they don't leave," he snarled.

He snapped his lips shut, hating that he'd let that last part escape. But now that it had, he couldn't stop the images of those he'd lost and the people they'd left behind from careening through his head.

Uncle Trent. His parents. Melissa.

"Besides," he ground out, "my reasons for divorcing Reagan stand. I'm doing her more harm than good remaining married to her. This way she won't be ostracized by *polite* Royal society or separated from her family. She'll have the chance to obtain her inheritance."

"Bullshit."

Ezekiel glared at his brother, who aimed one right back at him.

"I call bullshit," Luke repeated through clenched teeth. "You're running scared. Like you have for the last eight years. You speak of Melissa and Mom and Dad like they were cautionary tales. Mom and Dad's marriage is a goal, not a warning. Their love was the epitome of courage, of sacrifice and love. And you shit all over that when you use them to justify your fears. Zeke." Luke clapped a hand over Ezekiel's shoulder and squeezed. "You're about to throw your future away over something that you have no control over. You're so worried about what could possibly happen. Yes, God forbid, Reagan could *possibly* die in a tragic accident like Melissa and Mom and Dad. But you could also possibly have a wife and family and be complete in a way you've never known or could dream of. She's worth the risk. *You're* worth the risk."

Ezekiel stared at his brother, but it was Reagan's words echoing in his ears.

You don't get to use me as an excuse for running scared and not owning your own shit.

I threaten that pain and guilt that you've become so comfortable carrying around it's now a part of you. Because to admit that I'm more than a charity case to you means you would have to deal with the reality that you stand in your own way of finding acceptance and love.

Jesus. Ezekiel closed his eyes, and Luke gripped his other shoulder, holding him steady.

He loved her.

He loved Reagan Sinclair Holloway with his heart. His whole being.

Because if he didn't, he wouldn't be so damn terrified of being with her. She was right. She threatened his resolve, his beliefs about himself, his determination to forbid anyone from getting too close. From loving too hard.

Yes, he'd failed.

But not by marrying Reagan.

He'd failed in keeping her out of his carefully guarded heart.

At some point, she'd infiltrated his soul so completely that she owned it. He couldn't evict her. And... he didn't want to.

Did he suddenly believe he was worthy of her? No, but her strength, her warrior spirit made him want to strive to be worthy.

Was he suddenly not afraid? No. He'd believed a man should be brave enough to love her without fear, and that man wasn't him. But he'd been wrong. A man should just be brave enough to love. The fear of losing her might not ever go away, but he couldn't let it rule his life.

That man, he could be.

Starting now.

"You're going after her, aren't you?" Luke asked, a smile spreading across his face.

"Yes," Ezekiel said, as a weight he hadn't even been aware of bearing lifted from his chest. "And if she'll have me, I'm bringing her home."

Eighteen

Reagan stood in the back of the long line that bellied up to the funky but trendy food truck Street Eats. Of all the trucks hawking their fare, this one had a constant stream of people, ready and eager to grab the upscale street food. The sign next to the menu proudly declared the owner Lauren Roberts's focus on organic and farm-to-table produce.

Lauren herself helped serve the food, and even through the serving window, Reagan could easily see the businesswoman's loveliness. The Cinderella Sweepstakes included a makeover for the charity ball along with the free ticket, but she didn't need one. Smooth, glowing skin, pretty brown eyes, dark hair that was pulled back into a ponytail at the moment, and curves that Reagan envied completed the picture of a beautiful, confident and successful woman.

Reagan waited until the line had dwindled to a couple of people before joining it. Once she reached the window, Lauren smiled at her.

"Hey there. How can I help you?"

Reagan returned the smile. "Actually, I was wondering if I could have a couple of minutes, Lauren? My name is Reagan Sinclair," she introduced herself. "I'm on the planning committee for this year's Texas Cattleman's Club masquerade ball. And it's my pleasure to tell you that you're the winner of the Cinderella Sweepstakes radio contest."

Surprise widened Lauren's eyes. "You're kidding?"

"No, all true. You've won a ticket and a free makeover," Reagan assured her.

"Hold on a second. I'll be right out."

True to her word, Lauren emerged from around the truck moments later holding two cups.

"Sweet tea on the house," she said, offering Reagan one of the drinks. Sipping from her own tea, Lauren shook her head. "I still can't believe I won! Can I be honest?"

"Of course." Reagan tasted her beverage and savored the cool, refreshing tea with a hint of mint. Good Lord, it was delicious. "Wow, this is good."

"Thanks." Lauren grinned. But the wattage of it dimmed a little as she led Reagan to a nearby bench. Sitting, she curled a leg under the other and twisted to face Reagan. "I'm a little embarrassed to admit this, but I didn't even enter. A friend did it for me." She huffed out a chuckle. "Still, I'm excited to win. I never expected to. And I can't really pass up this opportunity to network with potential customers and investors. And shoot." She held up her hands, that grin tugging at the corner of her mouth again. "What woman doesn't enjoy a makeover?"

"A free one at that," Reagan teased. "Not that I think you need one. You're lovely just as you are."

"That's nice of you to say, but no." Lauren nodded, her eyes gleaming. "I'm looking forward to some changes."

"Well, then I'm glad I'm the one who could bring you the good news. And I'm looking forward to seeing you at the ball."

"Thanks, Ms. Sinclair," Lauren said, rising from the bench.

"Reagan." She stood as well, smiling. "Please call me Reagan. And thank you again for the tea."

"You're more than welcome." Lauren glanced over at the food truck where the line of customers had lengthened again. "I should get back. Thanks again, Reagan." Waving, she retreated back to her truck.

Reagan paused to finish her beverage, then headed toward her car across the street. A sense of accomplishment filled her. It was always awesome when good things happened to good people. And though she'd just met the other woman, Lauren seemed honest, hardworking and nice. Reagan looked forward to seeing her at the ball—

She stumbled to a halt. Shock swelled and crashed over her, momentarily numbing her.

Too bad she couldn't stay that way.

Already, the hurt and anger started to zigzag across that sheet of ice, the fissures growing and cracking. All at the sight of Ezekiel leaning against her car.

God, it wasn't fair. Not at all.

After the way he'd basically cast her aside, the only

emotions bubbling inside her should be fury and disdain. She might have walked away, but he'd let her. Without the slightest fight. That, more than anything, relayed how he felt about her.

Yet beneath the fury, there was also gut-churning pain and grief, for how not just their marriage but their friendship had ended.

And the ever-present need… Just one look at his tall, powerful body wrapped in one of his perfectly tailored suits—this one dark blue—and that handsome, strong face with those smoldering green eyes… Just one look, and she couldn't stem the desire or the memories that bombarded her, both decadent and cruel.

Slowly, he straightened, and she forced her feet to move and carry her across the street. Over the short distance, the anger capsized all the other emotions roiling inside her like a late-summer Texas storm. If he'd come to see if she was all right after he'd broken her heart, he could go straight to hell. She didn't need his pity. And she refused to be a balm that he could smooth over his self-imposed guilt.

No, thank you.

She'd wanted to be his wife, not an act of reparation.

"What are you doing here, Zeke?" she asked, voice purposefully bland, even though it belied the knots twisting in her belly or the constriction of her heart.

"Looking for you," he said simply, his gaze roaming over her face. Almost as if he were soaking in every detail.

Mentally, she slapped down that line of thinking. It could only lead to the seed of hope she'd desperately tried to dig up sprouting roots.

"After handing my ass to me in a sling, Harley told me where you were."

Okay, so Reagan and Harley needed to have a serious *come to Jesus* talk about consorting with the enemy. Or since the enemy was Harley's cousin, at least giving the enemy classified information.

"Well, you've seen me." Reagan sidestepped him and reached for the door handle. "Now if you don't mind, I have a meeting." Not a lie, she had an appointment with a realtor to find land for the girls' home she planned on building.

"Reagan," Zeke murmured, lifting a hand toward her. But when she arched a brow, daring him to complete the action, he lowered it and slid it into his pocket.

Self-preservation demanded he not touch her in any way. Her mind asserted she could withstand the contact, but her heart and her body? No, they were decidedly weaker when it came to feeling those magnificent hands on her.

"Reagan," he said again. "I know I don't have the right to ask you for it, but can I have just a couple of minutes? I want—"

"Let me guess. You want to apologize. You never meant to hurt me. And you would like to find a way to be friends again." She inhaled, bracing herself against that wash of fresh pain. But damn if she would let him see it. "Apology accepted. I know. And no. Not right now."

She went for the door handle again. But his fingers covered hers, and she stilled, the *don't touch me* dying a quick and humiliating death on her tongue. She couldn't speak, couldn't move when her nerve endings sizzled as if they were on fire.

He shouldn't affect her like this. Shouldn't ignite this insatiable, damn near desperate need for him. How many years before it abated? Before her body forgot what it felt like to be possessed by him?

She feared the answer to that.

"Please, sweetheart," he murmured, removing his hand, then taking a step back. "Hear me out, then I'll leave you alone."

"Fine," she bit out, conceding. Only because she suspected he wouldn't budge before having his say. And the sooner they got this done, the sooner she could drive away and pretend she didn't ache for him. Both her heart and her body. Just to be on the safe side though... She took another step back. "Just...don't touch me again."

"I won't," he promised.

She pretended not to see the flash of pain in his eyes.

"Reagan." He shifted his gaze away from her, squinting in the distance before refocusing on her. "I wanted you to know that Miles contacted Gracie. He was able to track her cousin's credit card purchases, and he found one at a convenience store for the same time the winning ticket was sold. That transaction was made out of state, not here in Royal. Miles managed to recover the store's video footage, and Alberto was there, on camera, paying for his purchase. Since it's scientifically impossible for him to be in two places at one time, he quickly dropped the claim against Gracie when Miles presented the evidence to him. So she's good."

"That's wonderful, Zeke. Thank you for having Miles look into it. I know Gracie has to be so delighted." Relief for her friend flowed through her, and she made a mental note to call her. But fast on the heels of that thought nipped another. "Is that what you wanted to tell me?"

It was *not* disappointment that crashed against her sternum. It wasn't.

"No," he said. "That was me stalling while I tried to gather my courage and ask you, no, beg you, to forgive me."

Beg. She blinked. No matter how hard she tried to conjure the image, she couldn't envision Ezekiel Holloway begging for anything.

"And though I'm asking for your forgiveness, I'm having a hard time extending it to myself. I was so wrapped up in my own pain, my own fear and guilt that I convinced myself I was doing what was best for you. When really, I was doing what was best for me. Well, what I believed was best for me. I couldn't have been more wrong."

Reagan sighed. "I've had twenty-six years of people making decisions based on what they think is best for me. And yet no one bothered asking my opinion on my life. Granted, I accept some of the blame for that, because I was afraid of rocking the boat, of not being loved. But I can't and won't allow that anymore, Zeke. From anyone. And I can't be with someone who respects me so little they think me incapable of making choices for myself."

"And you shouldn't settle for that, Reagan. Anyone who underestimates you is a fool. Like I was," he added softly. "Not that I ever underestimated your strength, your intelligence or drive. No, I misjudged your affect on me, my life…my heart."

"I… I don't understand."

"I didn't either. Until today. I thought I could put you

in this box and compartmentalize you in my life. But you…" He breathed a chuckle. "You can't be contained. You're this force that's fierce and powerful but one people usually don't see coming because it's wrapped in beauty, grace and compassion. I didn't stand a chance against you, Ray. And that's what had me running scared. I fought against the hold you had on me with everything in me because, sweetheart, you scare me. Loving you, having everything that is you, then possibly losing you? I couldn't bear it."

Loving you. Those two words echoed in her head, gaining strength like a twister. Wrecking every possible thought in its path except one. *Loving you.*

Oh God, no. Hope, that reckless, so-damn-stubborn emotion, dug in deep, entrenched itself inside her. She closed her eyes, blocking out his face. But she couldn't shut her ears. And they listened with a need that terrified her.

"I took the coward's way out before," he continued, shifting forward and erasing some of the space between them. "But now, I'm here, telling you that I'm no longer living in the past. Not when you're my future."

"Zeke, stop," she whispered, opening her eyes. Because she couldn't take any more. Love for this man pressed against her chest, threatening to burst through. No fear. That had no place between them anymore. She just wanted…him. He'd taken a risk by coming to find her and lay his heart out for her. And she could do no less but the same. Life, love—they required risk. Because the reward… God, the reward stared her in the face.

"Okay, sweetheart," he murmured, dragging a hand over his head. "I'll go, but one more thing. Some investments paid off for me, and they were substantial. Enough to no longer put your dream of a girls' home here in Royal on hold. Half of those earnings are yours. It's not a settlement. If we're going to divorce, you'll have to file the papers. I'll respect whatever you decide, but I can't let you go not knowing what I want. You. A real marriage. A family."

"I don't want your money, Zeke," she said. Pain flickered in his gaze, but he nodded. "No, you don't understand. I don't need it. All I need—all I want—is you. Us."

"What?" he rasped. "You mean…"

"Yes, I love you. With everything in me, I love you," she whispered.

"Sweetheart." He stared at her, his breath harsh and jagged. "Please give me permission to touch you."

"Yes. God, yes."

Before she finished speaking, he was on her, his hands cupping her face, tipping her head back. A heady wave of pleasure coursed through her as his mouth crushed hers, seeking, tasting…confirming.

"I thought…" He groaned, rolling his forehead against hers. "I thought I'd lost you. I love you, Reagan Holloway. You're mine, and I'm never letting you walk away from me again."

"Promise?"

"Promise," he swore, pressing a hard, passionate kiss to her lips.

"Then take me home and prove it," she said, laughing, unable to contain the joy bubbling inside her. And she didn't even try to contain it. "But we have to make a stop first. I'd love to have you with me for it." She couldn't imagine beginning this project of love without the love of her life.

"Fine," he agreed, grasping her hand and tugging her away from her car. "We'll take my car, then come back for yours." When they stopped next to the Jaguar, he tossed her the keys.

She gaped at him. Then at the metal she'd reflexively caught. Then back at him.

"Oh my God. You must really love me," she gasped.

Laughing, he rounded the hood of the car. The hood that he'd made love to her on.

"Forever, Ray."

* * * * *

**WE HOPE YOU ENJOYED
THIS BOOK FROM**

HARLEQUIN
DESIRE

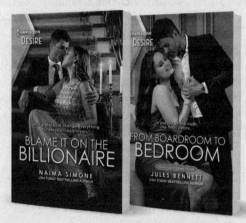

*Luxury, scandal, desire—welcome to
the lives of the American elite.*

Be transported to the worlds of oil barons, family dynasties,
moguls and celebrities. Get ready for juicy plot twists,
delicious sensuality and intriguing scandal.

6 NEW BOOKS AVAILABLE EVERY MONTH!

HDHALO2020

COMING NEXT MONTH FROM

⬡ HARLEQUIN

DESIRE

Available October 6, 2020

#2761 BILLIONAIRE BEHIND THE MASK
Texas Cattleman's Club: Rags to Riches
by Andrea Laurence

A Cinderella makeover for busy chef Lauren Roberts leads to an unforgettable night of passion with a masked stranger—commanding CEO Sutton Wingate. But when the masks come off and startling truths are revealed, can these two find happily-ever-after?

#2762 UNTAMED PASSION
Dynasties: Seven Sins • by Cat Schield

After one mind-blowing night together, bad boy photographer Oliver Lowell never expected to see Sammi Guzman again. Now she's pregnant. Passion has never been their problem, but can this black sheep tame his demons for a future together?

#2763 TEMPTATION AT CHRISTMAS
by Maureen Child

Their divorce papers were never filed! So, Mia Harper tracks down her still-husband, Sam Buchanan, aboard his luxury cruise liner. Two weeks at sea tempts them into a hot holiday affair...or will it become something more?

#2764 HIGH SOCIETY SECRETS
The Sterling Wives • by Karen Booth

Star architect Clay Morgan knows betrayal. Now he keeps his feelings—and beautiful women—at bay. Until he meets his new office manager, Astrid Sterling. Their sizzling chemistry is undeniable, but will a secret from her past destroy everything they've built?

#2765 THE DEVIL'S BARGAIN
Bad Billionaires • by Kira Sinclair

The last person Genevieve Reilly should want is charming jewelry thief Finn DeLuca—even though he's the father of her son. But desire still draws her to him. And when old enemies resurface, maybe Finn is exactly the kind of bad billionaire she needs...

#2766 AFTER HOURS REDEMPTION
404 Sound • by Kianna Alexander

A tempting new music venture reunites songwriter Eden Voss with her ex-boyfriend record-label executive Blaine Woodson. He wronged her in the past, so they vow to keep things strictly business this time. But there is nothing professional about the heat still between them...

YOU CAN FIND MORE INFORMATION ON UPCOMING HARLEQUIN TITLES,
FREE EXCERPTS AND MORE AT HARLEQUIN.COM.

HDCNM0920

SPECIAL EXCERPT FROM

ⒽHARLEQUIN
DESIRE

*A tempting new music venture reunites songwriter
Eden Voss with ex-boyfriend Blaine Woodson, a record
label executive. He wronged her in the past, so they vow
to keep things strictly business this time. But there is
nothing professional about the heat still between them...*

Read on for a sneak peek at
After Hours Redemption *by Kianna Alexander.*

Singing through the opening verse, she could feel the smile coming over her face. Singing gave her a special kind of joy, a feeling she didn't get from anything else. There was nothing quite like opening her mouth and letting her voice soar.

She was rounding the second chorus when she noticed Blaine standing in the open door to the booth. Surprised, and a bit embarrassed, she stopped midnote.

His face filled with earnest admiration, he spoke into the awkward silence. "Please, Eden. Don't stop."

Heat flared in her chest, and she could feel it rising into her cheeks. "Blaine, I..."

"It's been so long since I've heard you sing." He took a step closer. "I don't want it to be over yet."

Swallowing her nervousness, she picked up where she'd left off. Now that he was in the room, the lyrics, about a secret romance between two people with plenty of baggage, suddenly seemed much more potent.

And personal.

Suddenly, this song, which she often sang in the shower or while driving, simply because she found it catchy, became almost autobiographical. Under the intense, watchful gaze of the man she'd once loved, every word took on new meaning.

She sang the song to the end, then eased her fingertips away from the keys.

HDEXP0920

Blaine burst into applause. "You've still got it, Eden."

"Thank you," she said, her tone softer than she'd intended. She looked away, reeling from the intimacy of the moment. Having him as a spectator to her impassioned singing felt too familiar, too reminiscent of a time she'd fought hard to forget.

"I'm not just gassing you up, either." His tone quiet, almost reverent, he took a few slow steps until he was right next to her. "I hear singing all day, every day. But I've never, ever come across another voice like yours."

She sucked in a breath, and his rich, woodsy cologne flooded her senses, threatening to undo her. Blowing the breath out, she struggled to find words to articulate her feelings. "I appreciate the compliment, Blaine. I really do. But…"

"But what?" He watched her intently. "Is something wrong?"

She tucked in her bottom lip. *How can I tell him that being this close to him ruins my concentration? That I can't focus on my work because all I want to do is climb him like a tree?*

"Eden?"

"I'm fine." She shifted on the stool, angling her face away from him in hopes that she might regain some of her faculties. His physical size, combined with his overt masculine energy, seemed to fill the space around her, making the booth feel even smaller than it actually was.

He reached out, his fingertips brushing lightly over her bare shoulder. "Are you sure?"

She trembled, reacting to the tingling sensation brought on by his electric touch. For a moment, she wanted him to continue, wanted to feel his kiss. Soon, though, common sense took over, and she shook her head. "Yes, Blaine. I'm positive."

Will Eden be able to maintain her resolve?

Don't miss what happens next in…
After Hours Redemption *by Kianna Alexander.*

Available October 2020 wherever
Harlequin Desire books and ebooks are sold.

Harlequin.com

Copyright © 2020 by Eboni Manning

HDEXP0920

Get 4 FREE REWARDS!

We'll send you 2 FREE Books <u>plus</u> 2 FREE Mystery Gifts.

Harlequin Desire® books transport you to the world of the American elite with juicy plot twists, delicious sensuality and intriguing scandal.

FREE Value Over $20

YES! Please send me 2 FREE Harlequin Desire novels and my 2 FREE gifts (gifts are worth about $10 retail). After receiving them, if I don't wish to receive any more books, I can return the shipping statement marked "cancel." If I don't cancel, I will receive 6 brand-new novels every month and be billed just $4.55 per book in the U.S. or $5.24 per book in Canada. That's a savings of at least 13% off the cover price! It's quite a bargain! Shipping and handling is just 50¢ per book in the U.S. and $1.25 per book in Canada.* I understand that accepting the 2 free books and gifts places me under no obligation to buy anything. I can always return a shipment and cancel at any time. The free books and gifts are mine to keep no matter what I decide.

225/326 HDN GNND

Name (please print)

Address   Apt. #

City   State/Province   Zip/Postal Code

Email: Please check this box ☐ if you would like to receive newsletters and promotional emails from Harlequin Enterprises ULC and its affiliates. You can unsubscribe anytime.

Mail to the **Reader Service:**
IN U.S.A.: P.O. Box 1341, Buffalo, NY 14240-8531
IN CANADA: P.O. Box 603, Fort Erie, Ontario L2A 5X3

Want to try 2 free books from another series? Call 1-800-873-8635 or visit www.ReaderService.com.

*Terms and prices subject to change without notice. Prices do not include sales taxes, which will be charged (if applicable) based on your state or country of residence. Canadian residents will be charged applicable taxes. Offer not valid in Quebec. This offer is limited to one order per household. Books received may not be as shown. Not valid for current subscribers to Harlequin Desire books. All orders subject to approval. Credit or debit balances in a customer's account(s) may be offset by any other outstanding balance owed by or to the customer. Please allow 4 to 6 weeks for delivery. Offer available while quantities last.

Your Privacy—Your information is being collected by Harlequin Enterprises ULC, operating as Reader Service. For a complete summary of the information we collect, how we use this information and to whom it is disclosed, please visit our privacy notice located at corporate.harlequin.com/privacy-notice. From time to time we may also exchange your personal information with reputable third parties. If you wish to opt out of this sharing of your personal information, please visit readerservice.com/consumerschoice or call 1-800-873-8635. **Notice to California Residents**—Under California law, you have specific rights to control and access your data. For more information on these rights and how to exercise them, visit corporate.harlequin.com/california-privacy.

HD20R2

SPECIAL EXCERPT FROM

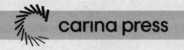

At Dallas's iconic luxury department store, you can feel good about indulging a little…or a lot. The staff is proud of their store. If you're one of them, you're three things: brilliant, boss and bomb.

Julia del Mar Ortiz moved to Texas with her boyfriend, who ended up ditching her and running back to New York after only a few weeks. Left with a massive— by NYC standards, anyway—apartment and the job opportunity of a lifetime, Julia is struggling… except that's not completely true…

Read on for a sneak preview of
Here to Stay
by Adriana Herrera,
available now from Carina Press.

He brought his cat to dinner.

I opened the door to my apartment and found Rocco holding the little carrier we'd bought for Pulga at the pet store in one hand and in the other he had a reusable shopping bag with what looked like his contribution for dinner.

"Hey, I know you said she was uninvited." His eyebrows dipped, obviously worried I'd be pissed at this plus-one situation. I wanted to kiss him so bad, I was dizzy. "But whenever I tried to leave the house, she started mewling really loud. I think she's still dehydrated."

Boy, was I in over my head.

I smiled and tried not to let him see how his words had actually turned me into a puddle of goo. "It's fine, since she's convalescent

CAREXPAHHTS0920

and all, but once she's back in shape, she's banned from this apartment."

He gave a terse nod, still looking embarrassed. "Promise."

I waved him on, but before I could get another word in, my mom came out of my room in full "Dia de Fiesta" hair and makeup. Holidays that involved a meal meant my mother had to look like she was going to a red carpet somewhere. She was wearing an orange sheath dress with her long brown hair cascading over her shoulders and three-inch heels on her feet.

To have dinner in my cramped two-bedroom apartment.

"Rocco, you're here. *Qué bueno.*" She leaned over and kissed him on the cheek, then gestured toward the living room. "Julita, I'm so glad you invited him. We have too much food."

"Thank you for letting me join you." Rocco gave me the look that I'd been getting from my friends my entire life, that said, *Damn, your mom is hot.* It was not easy to shine whenever my mother was around, but we were still obligated to try.

I'd complied with a dark green wrap dress and a little bit of mascara and lip stain, but I was nowhere near as made-up as she was. Except now I wished I'd made more of an effort, and why was I comparing myself to my mom and why did I care what Rocco thought?

I was about to say something, anything, to get myself out of this mindfucky headspace when he walked into my living room and, as he'd done with my mom, bent his head and brushed a kiss against my cheek. As he pulled back, he looked at me appreciatively, his gaze caressing me from head to toe.

"You look beautiful." There was fluttering occurring inside me again, and for a second I really wished I could just push up and kiss him. Or punch him. God, I was a mess.

Don't miss what happens next...
Here to Stay *by Adriana Herrera*
*available wherever Carina Press books
and ebooks are sold.*

CarinaPress.com

Copyright © 2020 by Adriana Herrera

CAREXPAHHTS0920